Beauty Within

By Jae El Foster

DCL Publications, LLC

© 2018 Jae El Foster

First Edition September 2018

DCL Publications
1033 Plymouth Dr.
Grafton, OH 44044

ISBN 978-1-7323742-7-0

This is a work of fiction. Names, characters, places and incidents are the product of the author's imagination, and any resemblance to any actual persons, living or dead, events, or locales, is entirely coincidental.

Cover design by Jae El Foster

Cover Model: CJ Hollenbach

PUBLISHED IN THE UNITED STATES OF AMERICA

"The more hidden the venom, the more dangerous it is." Margaret of Valois

Dedicated to those that yearn for a Happily Ever After.

1

The castle was prominent as the backdrop behind the tiny village. At the top of a hill on a dead plot of dirt and rock, the castle stood with defiance and crumbling pride. It was crafted of dark stone and rotted wood, and no tree around it showed any sign of life. It was often said throughout the small village below that the castle was haunted by centuries old ghosts, but everyone knew this as myth, as the castle was no more than a hundred and a half years old and any respectable ghost would haunt a castle with history and due reason for the presence. Everyone in the village knew that.

The village, if to be named, was Foliage, as during the spring and summer this was the most beautiful hidden-away spot anywhere between the tropics and the desert. Flowers and trees of all types budded and bloomed with the softest whites and pinks known to man. Hues of blues and violets and patches of oranges and bright, festive greens fluttered about the village with such delicacy and freedom, adding stellar life to this very much idyllic land. Every cottage and every shop spoke of taste and splendor. From the baker to the florist to the man with the cart who sold hand-carved wooden swords, bears and other childish toys at the edge of the town market, Foliage was, truly, enchanting.

For the most part, each person in the village seemed to get along rather well, and they all knew each other as family. When one would have a celebration or a holiday, all were free to join in. There was not a better place in the world that Natalie Wills could have imagined growing up. With her arms crossed over the ledge of her window, she stared out into the breathtaking world outside, remembering the many joys she had over the years. All too often as a young girl, she had ventured through the woods behind her home, ignoring her parents' wishes and enjoying the freedom of childhood, running spritely from tree to tree and imagining that they were all lively creatures filled with miraculous tales of wonder and magic. She had often played the princess with her friends, pretending that one of their homes was the castle at the time and she was royalty. All of the boys gladly played her servants, and each fought to be her prince. Even in childhood, Natalie had been an incredibly beautiful daughter of the earth.

When Natalie became a teenager, she only became more unruly. Her parents decided very early that Natalie had to be shown some type of discipline, so she was sent to a tutor during the day, learning as an apprentice the workings of the needle and thread, the spinning wheel, and how to prepare an excellent roasted boar. Yet, when her studies would end and Natalie was free to roam for the day, she would again play her role of the overly-adventurous young woman and lure the peasant boys with her charm and ever-growing beauty. She did, however, hold on to her chastity, which was a feat that she was currently very proud of.

"Daydreaming again, daughter?" she heard the voice call from behind her, startling her, and she sat up and turned with a laugh.

"Father, you startled me! I was simply enjoying this beautiful day." She beckoned her father to join her. "Look at it, Father. Isn't it the most beautiful thing you've ever seen? Smell that air!"

"It's more than apparent that spring is not far behind," he noted wisely, taking a brief glance with his daughter and taking in a deep breath of the crisp, floral scented air. "Your mother's roses should be lovely this season."

Natalie took her father's hand lovingly into her own and gave it a gentle squeeze, glancing for a brief moment into the strong dark orbs of his eyes before looking back out the window.

"You know... for at least the last ten years, I've found you right here... on this very day each time... staring out into the world with the same wonder and amazement as you are right now." Hiram Wills stated as he offered his daughter's hand a squeeze in return. "Always on your birthday... I know you must look out the window more than that, but I always seem to catch you on your birthday."

"Oh, Father… you're such a sentimental. It's no wonder you're so well loved in town."

"I'm so well loved because I am the only man in town who sells perfumed candles, my dear. The women love them!"

"I'm sure you've made a lord of the house angry a time or two," Natalie laughed.

"So be it! It puts food on our table, doesn't it?"

"You have a point. Besides, Mother seems quite fond of your candles. Why, if I were to come home someday and not smell one burning, I would think something terrible must have happened!"

Father joined her in this laugh, each now smelling the faint scent of a cinnamon perfumed candle burning in the back of the four room cottage.

"Would you like to accompany me to town, Natalie? It's about time to open shop for the day. Perhaps you could do a little shopping…"

"You're willing, and even offering, to let me shop?" she questioned in surprise. "This is definitely a first."

"It's not every day when a father has a daughter turn eighteen, Natalie. You're not my little girl anymore… you haven't been my little girl for a long, long time now."

"I'll always be your little girl," she replied fondly, kissing her father on the cheek. "And I'll accept your offer. Willem Grillis is also turning eighteen this week, and his parents are hosting a ball in his honor. I could definitely use a new dress if I'm to mingle with that crowd..." Suddenly, her mood changed to sadness and she lowered her eyes down to the sill of the window.

"Daughter," Hiram whispered as he lifted her chin with the thumb of his hand, "you are beautiful just as you are... the most beautiful girl in the village. If those people are going to judge you so harshly for the clothing on your body and not for your personality or natural charm... then why do you wish to go to this ball so badly?"

"Oh, Father... don't you see?" she pleaded, turning away from both her father and the window and crossing through to the center of her tiny bedroom. "A boy like Willem is the answer to a girl like me's problems. I mean... if I were to marry a boy that lived inside of the village..."

"You'd be stuck here," her father answered plainly... knowingly.

"Father, I didn't mean it like that."

"But it's true. You would be stuck here. Little to no chance of seeing and exploring the world... You deserve every opportunity that you can get, and you have my blessings and more to have the seamstress create you the perfect gown for this weekend."

"Father!" she exclaimed and rushed back to Hiram, embracing him in a tight hug. "You're just the greatest!"

"I have but one request," he announced as he broke the hug.

"What's that, Father?"

"That, if things should happen to… work out, and if you and this Willem lad should happen to wed and marry someday…"

"Yes?"

"You marry for love, not for money."

"Father…" Natalie breathed with a pleasant smile, "I say it again. You're such a sentimental."

"Natalie!" Mother cried in her loud but loving voice from the back of the house. "I have a list if you're going to town with your father!"

"I'm coming, Mother!" she replied giddily. Then, turning back to her father, she replied, "Worry not, Father. I guarantee that when love calls me, I will answer. But until then…"

"Until then, my daughter, explore the world. It can't do much harm."

"Natalie!" Mother called again, her voice just a tad bit higher. "Come here, daughter! I know you. You'll disappear and never know what to get for me!"

"Coming, Mother!" she called back again, finding it impossible not to laugh. Hiram, too, enjoyed the humor, knowing first hand of his dear wife's lack of patience and her overly anxious personality.

In the back room of the cottage which doubled as her parents' bedroom and their accounting office, Roselyn Wills sat at the small oak table, penning out her brief but thorough list onto a torn sheet of parchment paper. When she finished her inscription, she placed the quill back in its base and turned to face her daughter. Roselyn had a glowing smile across her face and a glimmer in her eyes.

"How's my beautiful girl this morning?" she asked pleasantly and in a lower tone than she usually spoke in.

"Just fine, Mother," Natalie whispered as she bent and kissed Roselyn's cheek. "How are you?"

"I'm perfect," she spoke softly. "It's my daughter's eighteenth birthday. My heart's overwhelmed."

"Oh, Mother..."

"I have something for you. I wanted to catch you before you left with your father."

"Yes, the shopping list. Of course."

"No, no. Not just the list, silly girl. Look there on the bed."

"Wrapped in the velvet?" Natalie questioned with strong curiosity.

"Unwrap it. Go ahead. I hope you like it."

Crossing over to the old rickety bed, Natalie stared down at the delicately wrapped package with thoughtful eyes. "I simply can't imagine what it is."

"Open it already! Are you trying to give your dear mother a stroke?" Roselyn pleaded, raising her voice back to the level that Natalie was more accustomed to.

She placed her hands atop the delicate blue velvet material, following its smoothness to the silky ribbon that was tied around it. Being as careful as possible, she took the two ends of the ribbon and began to pull, watching as the silk bow unfolded before her eyes. The ribbon dropped down into blissful layers of silky rose-colored bliss, spreading across the blue of the velvet.

"It's all so lovely…"

"That's the bow, dear," Mother answered quickly. "The gift is inside the packaging."

"I know that!" Natalie exclaimed laughingly. "I'm simply trying to enjoy the whole act of it all… the fabric and the ribbon and the way the bow was formed…"

"Would you just open it already? Your father's got to get to the market and I'm eager!"

"Yes, Mother," she laughed again, not in the least offended by her mother's impatient request. All of Foliage knew of Roselyn's downfalls and lack of social graces. She and Hiram were perfectly paired in many ways, but in just as many ways they were perfect opposites.

Continuing with the unwrapping, she pulled the ribbon completely free and set it beside the velvet wrapped package. She swallowed hard as her fingers touched the lining of the blue velvet, spreading it with gentle ease, as if afraid of damaging it. Mother knew that velvet was Natalie's favorite fabric, and this filled the maturing daughter with emotional pride. A tear drifted down her cheek as she turned the fold of the fabric over once more.

She had to take a step back. With a deep sigh, she placed a quivering hand across her heart and felt more tears ready to burst out into the open. Natalie held the tears back with determined force, but she showed her astonishment with a sudden gasp and a brief, sentimental cry.

"Mother!" she bellowed, staring down in amazement at the most beautiful white lace ball gown she had ever seen. The collar, cuffs, and bottom hem were all lined in cream-colored pearls, and beneath the delicately stitched cream lace, a white silk lining filled the inside, showing through the exterior holes of the lace. "It's… it's beautiful!"

Roselyn watched with a mother's joy as her daughter pulled the gown off of the bed and held it before her, measuring it against herself for size and fit. Perhaps the most intriguing and elaborate section of the gown was the layers and folds of the flowing skirt, which seemed to have a fullness that had no end.

"I know you wanted a new gown for the ball," Roselyn stated softly, lowering her tone to a more reasonable level. "I worked on this one for the last six weeks. I understand if you still want to have the town seamstress make you one, but you have this one for whatever occasion you choose to wear it."

"Mother, no other gown could compare to this one! It will be the most beautiful gown at the ball! I'm sure to win Willem's heart in this!"

Roselyn and Hiram watched their daughter with a joy that they would always remember fondly. The cost of materials for the gown had set them back quite a bit, and each had to work extra jobs in order to pay off the debt. With their steady but limited incomes, there was simply no extra money to spend. Yet, this was their Natalie, and so they spent anyway. The look on their daughter's face was more than enough reward for the proud, humble parents.

"I suppose now there's no sense in you going to the market with your old father, is there?" Hiram spoke up, noticing the time and the fact that the market had now been open for fifteen minutes and his shop was still locked.

"Oh, but Father," she began, eying the old man coyly as she sat the dress carefully back on the bed. "I still need a mask. It is a masquerade ball, after all."

"When those Grillises go out, they really go out, don't they…" Mother sneered with just a hint of jealousy.

"Do you think Madame Howell would have something, Father?" Natalie asked curiously, almost afraid of speaking the question, due to Madame Howell's reputation throughout the village.

"Madame Howell?" Hiram responded with a raised eyebrow. "Well… do you really think it's best to associate with such a character?"

"That's silly, Father. Madame Howell is a lovely woman!"

"She's a witch," Roselyn responded with a stern nod of the head. "Plain and simple. Everyone knows that witches can bring nothing but bad."

"Madame Howell doesn't have a bad bone in her withered old body!" Natalie smirked in retaliation. "She's been nothing but kind to me - always saying hello in the market and never failing to ask about you both. She has a heart of gold!"

"She's a witch," her mother repeated.

"I don't believe you, Mother. I simply don't. She may seem a bit queer at times, but she means no harm."

"She has snakes and skulls in her shop," Father noted, though his tone did not change. He showed no sign of swaying in the direction of either woman's view. "Yet, she's been in this village longer than any of the rest of us. She is our town elder. It is important to show her courtesy and respect."

"I never said there wasn't," Mother continued. "I simply stated that she's a witch... which she is."

"Either way," Natalie huffed, "I'm going. I know she has a mask that is just for me in that shop of wonders of hers, and I'm going to buy it before some other girl does and snatches it out from under me."

"You have to admit one thing, Roselyn," Hiram pointed out to his wife. "She has your spunk and determination."

"That's for sure," Roselyn grunted and then brought a smile back to her lips. Looking back to Natalie, she spoke softly again. "Happy birthday, dear daughter. I'm sure you'll be beautiful in whatever you find."

"The dress is more than beautiful, Mother - it's perfect!" Natalie cheered, shifting her mood to pleasant again, and leaning down to kiss Roselyn against her cheek.

"Okay, then," Hiram announced with a clearing of his

throat. "I'm late for work, so either you follow along later or you come with me, but either way I am going now."

"Coming, Father!" she announced, rushing to her father's side. Glancing back at her mother, she added, "Father gave me permission to shop today, Mother! He actually gave me permission!"

"Go easy on the dear old man," Roselyn warned her child. "With you, he might not have known what he was getting himself into."

"Oh, pooh, Mother," Natalie grinned, tossing a hand in Roselyn's direction and following Hiram out of the room. "Father knows me well."

"All too well, I'm afraid," Hiram announced humorously as they hurried toward the front door and out into the bright pre-spring morning sunshine.

Settling back in the clumsy wooden chair, Roselyn turned back to the desk before her. Then, shaking her head, she sighed with a grunt. "That girl," she whispered, eying the forgotten shopping list, still sitting on the desktop. "She'd forget her head if the bloody thing weren't attached."

2

Her father's shop – otherwise known simply as Wax – was the second shop on the right of the cobblestone street once they stepped into the marketplace. Today, the marketplace seemed busier than normally, and peasants, servants, children, and peddlers filled nearly every foot of the broad street. Hiram had no time this morning to shop with his daughter, although he would have enjoyed nothing more. So, despite his worries of sending her off to Madame Howell's alone, he kissed her goodbye on the steps of his shop and opened his door for business. Natalie was not two steps away before it became overwhelmed with eager customers.

Today would prove a good business day for her father, she knew, and this pleased her so. Natalie was not a fool. She did most of the shopping for the family and knew more or less how much the fabric alone for her new dress had cost her dear parents. And then the pearls… It was a bit overwhelming for the young daughter, who knew that she was perhaps the most blessed woman in the marketplace today.

Then for her parents to agree to let her shop for a new mask for the ball… Natalie knew that a dress would have set them back a good bit, so she hadn't dared mentioned the need for a mask. But when she saw the beautiful dress that her mother had crafted for her, she simply could not help but mention the mask, and of course, Madame Howell.

"They certainly must think me grown now," she mumbled to herself as she worked her way toward Madame Howell's Shoppe of Wonders. She could see even from here that there was not a crowd at the old woman's shop. In all her eighteen years, she could never remember there ever being a crowd there. How the woman managed to survive was well beyond her mind's conception.

Stepping up to Madame Howell's crumbling front steps, Natalie took a deep breath and felt a cool chill encompass her body. This was odd, she thought, as it was rather warm out today for not even being spring yet. But then again, it was the end of winter, and chills and breezes were to be expected.

Still, she had not felt a breeze - only the chill.

Brushing this cold feeling away, she placed her hand on the rickety knob of the door and pushed the large wooden block open.

"Madame Howell?" she asked calmly, poking her head into the dim, dusty shop of curiosities. She had only actually been inside the shop a handful of times in her life, but each time seemed new and different – although every piece within was old and ancient. There were costumes of all sorts and from any period of time the young woman could imagine, and the artwork was always brilliant and outstanding, but more often than not, created by someone that Natalie had never heard of before. The same was to be said for the sculptures, weaponry, charms, and nearly everything else contained inside this small but overwhelming shop. Natalie knew that if given the opportunity she could have spent all day or night here, mystified by each and every treasure that surrounded her.

"Natalie Wills," the old withered voice called as pleasantly as possible from the back of the shop. "Come in, dear. I've been expecting you."

"You have?" Natalie asked as she stepped fully into the shop and shut the door behind her.

"It is your birthday, is it not?" the old woman asked in a long breath as she stood from her shadowed chair and stepped out into a bit of light. She had aged a bit since Natalie had last seen her, but the young woman recognized the friendly glimmer in the old woman's eye.

"Why, yes, ma'am. I'm eighteen today."

"Eighteen. That's a wonderful age to be. A very cherished number. You should do something to celebrate this milestone."

"Well," Natalie began, smiling a bit and rolling her eyes up to the ceiling, "Willem Grillis's parents are throwing a masquerade ball in his honor. He, too, is turning eighteen this week."

"And you are going to this ball?" the withered old woman asked as the glimmer in her eye seemed to catch a spark and ignite.

"Oh, yes! I've been looking forward to it since I received my invitation. Mother made me a beautiful gown to wear, but it's a masquerade ball which means I need to find a mask. That's my reason for visiting today, Madame Howell. I was hoping you might have something here that would suit me. The dress is cream lace and white silk with cream pearls around the collar and cuffs."

"It sounds enchanting," Madame Howell breathed slowly. "And I think I may have something here just as enchanting that will suit you for all of your needs."

"Oh, Madame Howell! That would be wonderful!"

"Give me a moment, child," the woman answered in her kindly old tone and raised finger as she turned away from Natalie, moving back into the shadows of the shop. "It is in the back room. I will return momentarily."

Natalie did not hear a door open or close, nor could she see a door at all. It was almost as if Madame Howell had walked through the wall, or simply into darkness. The young woman found this quite curious, but she did not allow it to plague her mind. She refused to admit that her parents had been right. She refused to admit that Madame Howell was a witch.

While she waited, she roamed through the shelves of curiosities and wonders that surrounded her. There were jars of herbs and spices that she had never heard of, except some of them seemed familiar from stories she'd read in books as a child. One shelf contained nothing but different forms of incense, and each smelled of something completely different. Having worked in her father's shop often and having been surrounded by more perfumes than she cared to admit, she felt amazed at the unusual and peculiar scents of the incenses - scents she had never before smelled.

Directly across from her, she spotted a stuffed monkey and nearly jumped. She had, at first glance, believed it to be alive, and she was not sure if that thought frightened her more or if it was the thought of being so close to a dead monkey that couldn't jump out at her. Either way, she moved away from it as quickly as possible.

"Natalie," Madame Howell called as she crept back into the room. "I found it. It's perfect for you. You could even say it was made for you."

"Okay, I'm coming," she responded, searching for a way back to the center of the shop without having to pass the monkey again, but finding no other options. Taking a deep breath, she hurried down the short aisle and lunged back into the center aisle, exhaling with a smile as she faced again Madame Howell.

"You are going to this ball to impress a man, yes?" the old

woman asked, holding her hands behind her.

"Well, I guess you could say that." Natalie blushed at the blunt honesty of the old woman's question. "I'm certainly going to try, anyway."

"Very good," the old crone replied. "Then what I have will suit you well." From behind her, she pulled a mask handcrafted from cream lace and white satin with cream pearls running all along the outer edges. It looked as if it had been made specifically to go with the gown her mother had crafted. The mask was a perfect match.

"Madame Howell," Natalie breathed - or *tried* to. "It's - it's a perfect match, Absolutely perfect!"

"I thought it might be," the old woman beamed, showing more expression than Natalie had ever seen in her before. "The mask is very old, Natalie. Wear it Saturday night and I guarantee you will meet your soul mate at that ball."

"I don't know if I'll meet my soul mate," the young girl confessed with a youthful smile, "but I do intend on getting a bit closer to Willem that night."

"If it's meant to be," the old woman warned, "it will happen."

"Oh!" Natalie choked suddenly as she remembered something very important. "My father - I forgot to get payment from him. I'll have to come back."

"Nonsense, child," Madame Howell laughed. "It is your birthday, after all. Consider the mask a gift."

"Oh, but I couldn't…"

"You could, and you shall," she responded slowly, handing the mask over to Natalie without a second thought about it. The young woman took it limply in her hands, astonished by Madame Howell's generosity.

"Thank you so much, Madame Howell. It's so perfect."

"Just wear it in good health and with good intentions, and you will do my old heart some good."

"Thank you again, Madame Howell," Natalie chimed, leaning over to kiss the short woman on her wrinkled cheek. This brought a smile to the old woman's face, who had probably not been shown affection from another human in at least three decades. "You don't know how much this means to me. Mother will be beside herself with amazement, too!"

"How are your parents, my dear?"

"They're fine, thank you. Father is busy at his shop today and Mother is doing some odds and ends. Their normal routines, I suppose."

"I imagine they are a bit tense over your birthday?"

"Well, I know that they spent more than they should

making that dress, and so they've had no time to themselves; extra work is commonly available here in Foliage, thankfully."

"Perhaps... perhaps your parents need something to help ease them this evening. It just so happens that I have a bottle of wine here with me that I think would be perfectly suited for their needs. I'd be willing to send it to them on the condition that they not know it came from me."

"Why's that, Madame Howell?" she asked, trying to take in her generosity.

"They think I'm a witch. They'd never drink it if they knew it came from a witch."

"You know about that?" Natalie questioned, expressing her shock.

"Of course, child. I am a witch. Everyone knows that. Now here," she laughed, reaching back into the shadows and pulling out a bottle without a label, filled with red liquid. "Take this to your parents. Just tell them someone gifted it to them in the marketplace. I guarantee they'll enjoy it."

"You're a witch?" Natalie questioned slowly as she took the bottle from the woman's thin hands.

"Don't question the obvious, Natalie. Just take your parents the wine, enjoy the mask, and let me know how the ball goes."

"I will," she promised, digesting the newfound information

and smiling, deciding that Madame Howell was still the friendliest woman in town – even if she was a witch.

She said her goodbyes to the kindly old woman and carried her new goods back out into the pre-spring sunshine. She no longer felt that odd chill as she crossed down the broken steps and onto the cobblestone street. All around her, people continued to shop madly through the marketplace, carrying on various conversations and haggling with stubborn merchants. Natalie laughed at the sight, finding it humorous after such an intense visit with Madame Howell.

Glancing down at the bottle in her hands, she wondered what exactly it was inside. Something told her that it wasn't wine, as Madame Howell had tried to convince her. Either way, she knew that the old woman would do nothing to cause her parents harm, and she trusted this instinct enough to follow through with the self-proclaimed witch's request. Her next stop was to be her father's candle shop.

The tiny bell above the door rang as Natalie entered, and Hiram barely had enough time to glance up from his counter and wave hello. Eight men and women surrounded him, eagerly awaiting him to fill their orders. It was the most Natalie could remember seeing all at one time, and it filled her with happiness.

"Do you need help?" she offered loudly over the chitchatting of the customers.

"Not a bit, dear!" he called back in a joyful tone. "I'm loving every minute of this."

"Somebody gifted you a bottle of wine, Father. Where should I place it?"

"Carry it home, Natalie! Mother and I will celebrate nicely tonight! Now, let father work."

"I'll see you soon, Father," she called proudly as she waved goodbye and stepped back out into the bustling marketplace.

It was now that she realized she had forgotten something very important this morning. Her mother's shopping list had slipped her mind entirely, and now a bit of rush and panic hit her as she began to start home. She would have to claim the list and make a second venture into the marketplace, and by that time all of the best goods would have already been picked through. Mother always preferred her shopping to be done early, when the best and freshest supplies were available for one's choosing. Gazing out into the mob of shoppers around her, she knew the best was long gone.

"No worries, dear daughter," she heard her mother's voice call from beside her. Glancing over, Natalie sighed at the sight of Roselyn and her shopping basket, already half-filled with goods. "I noticed right away that you forgot the list, but I decided to give you the day off."

"My apologies, Mother," Natalie smiled with remorse. "I was just so anxious to find a mask."

"And did you find one?"

"Like you won't believe," she chimed, pulling the mask from under her arm and showing her mother the perfect match to the dress she had created.

"Oh, my." Roselyn sighed, unable to resist the smile that grew over her lips. "It is perfect, isn't it?"

"It's more than perfect, Mother! It's like it was made for this very occasion!"

"Perhaps it was."

Natalie noticed the cock of her mother's eyebrow with her comment and allowed her own smile to grow a tad larger.

"I told you, she is just a kind old woman."

"She's a witch."

"I know."

"She told you?" Roselyn asked with an 'I told you so' smirk.

"She wondered why I was surprised," Natalie admitted with humor. "Then, I guess I just wasn't surprised anymore."

"That was witchcraft."

"That was me using common sense, Mother. I was gifted

with a little of that, you know."

"I know, dear daughter."

"And, speaking of gifting, if you could put this in your basket," the daughter added, offering Roselyn the bottle of wine. "This was gifted to you and father a little while ago as I passed through the market."

"Oh…" she hesitated before finally accepting the wine. "How nice. I could use something to kick back with this evening, I tell you. Does your father know about this yet? Perhaps I could keep it to myself and nip it every now and then."

"I saw him first."

"Bah…" she shrugged, settling the wine into her basket. "Ah, well. I'm sure we won't drink it all tonight anyway, but I've got a list of chores a mile long, so I'm sure a good bit of the brew will be gone by bed."

"Okay, well… I guess I can wander now for a bit?"

"Have fun, Natalie. Just be home for supper. I'm preparing your favorite tonight."

"I can't wait!" she expressed, waving goodbye as her mother smiled and headed back into the thick of the marketplace shoppers.

Natalie felt ten times better now after having spoken with her mother and knowing that the day's shopping was being handled. She was free to roam about, but there was a simple problem with this. There was nowhere in particular that she currently wanted to roam.

Passing person after person – women with their children, merchants chasing unruly youths, peasants who simply happened to be out and about – she ambled her way to the center of the old but pristine cobblestone street and crossed over to the village fountain. The center statue of the fountain was of Aphrodite, the goddess of love, and it reflected a passion and beauty that seemed to surge through this village that the rest of the world often seemed to have forgotten. Aphrodite stood atop a mass of shells and stones with water following through the mouths of the golden fish and back into the flow of the fountain's pool. People often tossed bits of gold into the fountain, honoring the gifts that they credited Aphrodite to have bestowed upon them. No one ever took from the fountain though. That meant instant damnation of one's soul – or so the village counsel often warned.

Taking off her slippers, Natalie stepped onto the short ledge of the fountain and stood tall over the thick of merchants and shoppers. She looked at each and every face as she gazed out into the crowd, as if searching for somebody but not knowing who. She gazed at every shop and cart, every cottage that could be seen in the distance. She stared at the small but dominate cathedral for a matter of time, briefly wondering what it looked like inside. She hadn't visited a mass since early childhood, when her father discovered that Sundays were the only days he could work in his shop without being distracted by customers and when her mother could finally rest after a week of hard chores and tasks. Natalie actually knew very little of the many things her mother did. Roselyn never spoke of work, and she never complained about it. She was, perhaps, the strongest woman that Natalie knew. She was Natalie's inspiration.

Deciding for now that the cathedral wasn't where her heart wanted to roam, she passed it over and continued her search. Then, prominently displayed on the horizon of the village, her eyes fell upon the old, crumbling castle that so many local myths and rumors had been based. Natalie had never actually seen anyone go to or from the castle, but many have claimed actual knowledge of the hideous monster that it contained within. Some said that it was a beast with deformities far from human, and others had specified that there was nothing at all human about the monster - that it had been created by some mad demon, sent to destroy anyone who came near the castle.

Natalie thought each of these ideas to be nonsense, but she couldn't help letting her curiosity overwhelm her. What was really trapped inside the walls of that castle? Her father had told her a tale once about a family that had inhabited those stone walls, and he had briefly mentioned a tragic ending to the family's lives. He hadn't gone into any more detail than that, deciding it best to not scar his daughter at the early age.

"Staring at the monster's castle?" Sarah St. John chimed in a rude tone as she approached Natalie from behind, nearly causing her to lose her balance on the ledge of the fountain. "You're not planning on going up there are you?"

Climbing down from the fountain, Natalie smiled as best she could at Sarah, who had played the role of her rival practically since birth. The two young women had a great distaste for each other.

"Is there really a monster there, do you think?" she asked, wondering how honest an answer she would get from her nemesis.

"He's not a real monster," corrected Victoria Luther, who accompanied Sarah here in the marketplace. "But in a way, yeah, he's about as big of a monster as they have around here!"

"And I hear that Willem's invited him to the ball on Saturday night!" added Sarah.

"No!" exclaimed her friend.

"Really, Natalie, the lad gives new definition to the term 'beast'."

"What's wrong with him?" she asked curiously, glancing

again at the dark castle on the hill.

"No one knows," continued Sarah. "Some say he was born a mutant with deformities of all sorts. I've never actually seen him. None of us have."

"But we will on Saturday," cheered Victoria.

"If he has the nerve to show," Sarah chastised.

"It's a costume ball," Natalie whispered, throwing her two cents in. "We'll never know if he's there or not."

"I won't be looking for him either way," Sarah continued. "I've got my sights set on Willem. Mother had a custom made gown created for me by one of the Sirs in France! I'm certain to be the eye-catcher of this masquerade ball."

Suddenly, Natalie felt herself grow rather ill and she excused herself from the company of her nemesis and her cohort. It was true that the dress her mother had made her was beautiful, but could it possibly complete with a Paris original? Willem would be able to smell the wealth and sophistication of Sarah, and he wouldn't even acknowledge Natalie's existence. The mere thought of this brought tears to her eyes, and once she was out of the marketplace and free to be emotional, she allowed herself to cry through her run. She hurried blindly in tears down a small empty road, passing by several cottages and small farms before becoming surrounded by the trees she used to find reassurance and comfort in during the days of her youth.

She realized in this instant that she was no longer the carefree Natalie that she once was. She had grown, matured, and become emotional over boys – even more so than before. She could not understand why, though. Why all of these tears over Willem? She knew that she did not love him, but it was the fact that Sarah was trying to claim him. That was what hurt Natalie the most. She knew she didn't have a chance against her.

Whereas Natalie was much more beautiful and pleasant, Sarah had a habit of giving the boys what they wanted the most.

That was something that Natalie simply was not comfortable doing… not until the sacred band was wrapped around her slender finger.

When she finally stopped running and her tears had run dry, she realized she had gone deeper into the woods than ever before. She stood at the foot of a rather large and ragged hill that seemed to climb higher into the air than any other in town. Natalie suddenly knew where she had run to. She was standing at the foot of the hill that led to the infamous castle that towered over the small village of Foliage. She had run straight to the one place she had never ventured before in her life, despite all she had heard about it.

"Will this be my demise?" she questioned lightly and began

up the rough hill. "Will my eighteenth birthday be my last? I can hear it now. 'Village Beauty Eaten Alive by Hideous Monster'. Sarah should enjoy that immensely."

She found that by climbing the hill, she worked off much of the angst that had filled her bones, and by the time she had reached the dusty, grim top, she somehow felt much better. She also noticed that between her frantic run and the climbing of the hill, she had lost all track of time, and if she were to make it home in time for supper as promised, she would have to turn back.

Still… she yearned for one – just one – peek inside the famously rumored castle.

"I'm all the way up here," she thought aloud. "I may as well. If I don't go inside, I'll regret it. Of course, it's quite possible that I'll just as much regret going inside."

Creeping as slowly and as quietly as possible, Natalie edged her way to the side wall of the castle, where the stench of moldy dampness hit her immediately. Touching upon the wall, she felt the dampness and pulled her hand away. The stickiness of slime remained until she wiped it off on the fabric of her dress. She took note of the green ivy that raced along the wall and wondered if it was possible that it was the cause of the damp slime.

A rustling sounded from beneath her foot and she took a leap back, sighing in relief at a twig that had snapped beneath her feet. In a place this grim, she had imagined nothing less than the most venomous snake.

Collecting herself, she continued her trek to the corner of the castle walls, where she cautiously turned to find the front lot of the structure empty. Soulless.

Soulless... she was not sure that she liked that word, but somehow it seemed fitting. Swallowing deep, Natalie began to turn the sharp-edged corner of the castle, growing closer to the entrance with each step. A look to her left showed the village down below, barely viewable through the thick of the fog. Whereas it was still sunny in Foliage, it was hard for Natalie to make out more than just a few cottages and a hint of the gold from Aphrodite's fountain from this distance and in the encasement of the fog.

"It's still so beautiful," she noted from her position, considering she was now against the grimmest backdrop of her small village. For a moment, she wondered if perhaps she could be seen from the marketplace. She had, herself, clearly viewed the castle from the ledge of the fountain. At that time, she had not noticed a bit of fog around the structure, and this made her realize the fog had risen with early dusk, and in an hour, it would encompass the town. More time had passed than she had realized.

Still, she could not resist the temptation of glancing inside the forbidden castle. She was so close. She would never forgive herself if she passed up this rare opportunity. Many of the townspeople claimed to have seen the monster and they told terrible tales of the occurrences in the castle, but none had ever admitted to having ventured inside. Natalie now considered the possibility that there was no monster... it simply did not exist. There was no mutated man, and there were no horrors. And in just a moment, she would find out for herself.

The door to the old castle was large and gray, braced with iron bolts and steel sheathing. The handle seemed heavy and imposing, but it proved quite easy as she offered it a push and the door slowly creaked open. A bit of dust flooded out and she covered her mouth to avoid breathing any in. Standing directly in front of the entrance, she stared inside, attempting to make out shapes and objects through the shadowed darkness.

"Hello?" she called, leery of entering without attempting to announce herself. Still, she felt a bit frightened at the possibility of a reply.

When a moment passed and she had not heard a mumble or a shriek, she took a brave step forward and entered into the imposing castle. The strong scent of musk and dampness filled her nose, but it was not an overwhelming stench and she found it somewhat easy to bear. Her ears finally picked up on one sound – the dripping of water from somewhere nearby. She assumed that it was from a leaky roof, but the leak made no sense as Foliage had not had a downpour in nearly three weeks. It had not snowed in eight weeks, and the sun had been warm enough to dry the land a hundred times over. Natalie allowed this peculiarity to slide for the moment, but she knew that she would consider it again later in the night.

Her eyes were adjusting as she began to make out some of the shapes and images that beckoned to her through the darkness. In the middle of a foyer that she considered had once been elegant, a grand piano waited under a shield of dust, beckoning some soul to relieve it of its cobwebs and tickle the ivories that had gone virtually rusty. Behind the piano was an even grander staircase that seemed to climb up into nothing but blackness. Natalie could not imagine ever having to climb such high, winding stairs in such a dim setting, and she put the fearful thought aside.

Crossing over to a sitting area, she took note of the once-white sheets that had grown dingy and gray with time. They sat strewn across many pieces of furniture – sofas, chairs, end tables… She wondered if the tables were marble-topped and if the sofas were nicely upholstered, but then she imagined that it did not matter either way.

Despite what Sarah had told her down by the fountain, Natalie knew that Willem had not sent an invitation for his ball to this castle. If he had, she knew that no one would be coming. This place had been long deserted. All of the signs were there. The castle was dying from lack of ownership, and there was no one here to restore it.

She imagined that at some point in her lifetime, she would watch this structure crumble completely from lack of care and upkeep, and then the town would no longer have it looming over them from atop the great, dead hill.

Well... she had done it. She had seen the inside of the castle. The dusty art on the walls... the busts and statures encased in cobwebs... the furniture covered in ghostly sheets... all dimmed in silent darkness. Now, at least, she could put an end to the horror stories that flooded around the building. There was no monster. There were no spooks. There was only dirt and spiders. Lots of dirt and spiders...

Turning back to the open door, she saw that the sun would be setting momentarily, and if she did not hurry, she had no hope of being home in time for supper. She hurried out of the castle, forgetting about the open door and rushing across the dirt lawn to the edge of the hill, where she began her rough climb down. All thoughts of her adventure were currently stored in her mind for remembrance later. For now, she had her mother to contend with.

* * * *

From the shadows of the castle foyer, a form crept out of his hiding. He stood tall and slender, donned in black satin pants, deerskin boots, and a mesh shirt. His long blond hair curled around his shoulders, dipping lower behind him to his back. He breathed softly, causing the strong muscles of his chest to rise and fall with each delicate breath. Then, with a huff, he straightened and inched out of the shadows and into the dim ray of sunlight that broke in through the open doorway. Lifting one of his chiseled arms, he brought a hand to his face, covering it as he stepped to the threshold. There he bent and lifted into his hand the lace and silk mask that the strange young woman had dropped in her hasty departure. Clutching it tightly, he moved to the door and pushed it shut with his shoulder. Then, bringing the mask to his face, he took in deep its scent. Clenching it to his chest, he rushed up the winding staircase at the back of the foyer and into the impossible darkness within his castle.

3

She rushed into the cottage with a breathless pant, exhausted from the tremendous workout she had just given her body. Hiram and Roselyn waited silently at the table, surrounded with foods that had been ready for nearly an hour. She wasn't impossibly late, but she was still late.

"Your birthday feast awaits you," her father announced lightly as she crossed to the table. "Did you show your mother your new mask?"

"My mask?" she questioned with sudden recognition of the fact that she was no longer holding it. "Oh no…"

"What's wrong?" Roselyn asked as she sipped her cider.

"I lost my mask… somewhere today." Tears filled the young woman's eyes as she sat heavily down in her chair and hung her head low. "How could I? That mask was so perfect too."

"Now, now, Natalie." Hiram comforted her with a hand to her shoulder. "It will be alright. We'll find you another mask for the ball."

"The ball is Saturday. This is Thursday. How will I ever find another one like it in time?"

"I could try to make you one," her mother announced in

straight-forward voice. "I still have some fabric left from your gown. I don't have any more pearls, but I'm sure I could make do."

"Oh, Mother, I couldn't ask you to do that. You do so much already. There's no way you would have time."

"I'm a mother, dear child. Mothers always have time for their children." Placing a hand upon her daughter's she squeezed it tenderly. "It may not be as beautiful or as magical as the one that Madame Howell gave you, but it will be made from love."

"Do you know where you may have lost it, dear?" Hiram asked her, engaging in the conversation.

"I have an idea..." she whispered, closing her eyes for a moment and remembering the dark castle and the musky, damp scent within. It must have been in her rush to leave when the mask fell from her hand, and in her anxiousness, she had not realized its departure, thus leaving it behind.

"So should I make you a new one, or are you going to attempt to retrieve your lost one?" Roselyn was growing impatient as she waited for a straight answer on if she had yet another task to do or not.

Thinking it over a bit, she softly nodded her head. "Yes, Mother, please. I would adore a homemade mask. I know it will be beautiful, and I don't see any chance of recovering my old one within the next two days."

"Very well then," Roselyn nodded with a half-smirk. In her heart, the woman had to admit a bit of jealousy over the mask that the town's witch had crafted for her. She knew that the old woman would have never done Natalie any harm, but this ball was the apple of Natalie's eye, and Roselyn wanted to be the one to make the event special for her.

Twenty minutes later, Natalie felt the exhaustion of her day set into her, and she excused herself from the table for early bed. Hiram and Roselyn seemed to not mind, as they were inching closer and closer to uncorking the bottle of wine that Madame Howell had sent along. Natalie did not know what the wine would do to her parents, but she imagined that it was a sight she need not see.

In her room, she shut the heavy wooden door and leaned her back against it, taking in a heavy, exhausted breath. She was still beating herself up mentally, angered that she had lost the gift that Madame Howell had presented her with. The mask had truly been one of a kind, and no matter the effort that her mother put into the new one, Natalie knew that it would not be the same. For one, it would not have the elegant pearls that captured her dress so beautifully. Secondly, it would not bring her the love of her life.

This was a silly bit of fantasy, she knew as she stepped away from the door and stared down at her bed. As she undressed, she closed her eyes and imagined the night of the ball, and how it would have been, had she not lost her special mask.

Willem Grillis would have spotted her as she walked in… the gown flowing around her feet… the mask perfectly placed against her pale face. The lush red of her hair would have trailed down over her bare shoulders, and she would have smiled at the future Lord of Grillis Manor, faltering him with her alluring gaze and irresistible sensuality. Willem would have gone to her then, saying not a word as he approached, but instead taking her by the hand and waist and leading her out onto the ballroom floor for her first dance of the evening. He would not have danced with another soul for the entire night. He would have been hers and hers alone. Once the night was over and the guests had begun to retreat to their homes, he would have kissed her, and he would have been hers forever…

"Ha!" she laughed, slipping into her nightgown and yawning with exhaustion. "If anyone, it will be Sarah leading him around the floor in her arms. She would never leave an ounce of happiness for anyone else."

Climbing into her bed, she turned down the kerosene lantern that her parents had lit for her before her arrival home, and she closed her eyes with heavy memories of the day plaguing her.

The castle was prominently placed in her mind, towering

high over any other thoughts that might have tried to sneak in. She remembered vividly what she had seen inside - the piano… the staircase… She even remembered the view of Foliage from atop the tall, dead hill, and the fog that had surrounded her.

Once again, she took concern in the possibility that someone had seen her while on the hill, gazing out over the village. But what if they had? What harm could have been caused by being seen on an adventure?

And it had been an adventure. No one that she knew of had ever dared step foot inside the forbidden castle, and she had proven herself braver than any other. In fact, she hoped that someone had seen her up on that hill. It would have been the proof she needed, as she knew that no one would ever believe she had entered the castle – especially alone.

She thought of the twisted staircase, and her mind was further filled with wonder. What other rooms did the mysterious castle hold, and where was the monster that was said to rule it?

"There were no monsters there," she mumbled, rolling over onto her side and snuggling further under her blanket. Although the day had been warm, it was still a few weeks until spring officially hit, and the chill of the night had begun to creep inside. "One can sense a monster, and I sensed no monsters inside of that castle. Spiders, perhaps, but no monsters."

Yawning through her muttering, she fell silent and drifted off to sleep.

* * * *

Outside, a wind fell over the sleeping Foliage, blowing hard through the trees and beating against every door and window shutter in its path. It blew with such harsh strength that the shutters in the sleeping Natalie's bedroom were forced open, and a bit of lightning streaked into the night, brightening the earth for only a moment in time.

In this moment, however, the lurking, shadowed creature outside could be seen, staring into the darkness of Natalie's bedroom.

He watched for a long period, letting the wind waft through his thick blond hair. He stood in the same clothes that he had worn earlier, when the beautiful sleeping intruder had invaded his castle. The sight of her had taken him for more than a surprise. It had been many years since another soul had last stepped foot inside of his domain. He was not accustomed to visitors, and as a rule, he did not care for them.

This one had been different though. Whether it had been her appearance, her scent, or the strength of her roaming character, he had allowed her to enter his castle, well aware that she had been creeping around the outside. He had watched her as she entered through the front, stepping into the damp, dark foyer and gazing around in sheer wonder and amazement.

This woman... this beautiful vixen... had managed to render him both shocked and pleased all at the same time. His heart had beat heavily when first seeing her climbing up the side of the hill, and it had fallen dead and crushed when she left the castle in haste. Now, staring at her through her bedroom window, he felt whole again. Alive. Frightened. Seeing her sleeping made him wish to be in the room with her... in the bed... holding her... holding another human being for the very first time...

Shaking his head, he sighed against the howl of the wind and looked down to his hands. In them, he held the mask that he had collected earlier, lost from the fleeing maiden's grip. Running a thumb over the smooth silk, the ripples of the lace, and the plump of the pearls, he allowed a thin smile to grace his shadowed lips then moved even closer to the window. The dark lord reached in through the open window and dropped the mask inside, watching it land safely on a small wooden table.

Before stepping back for his departure, he glanced once again at the sleeping beauty. He knew not her name, but he had come up with many aliases for her. Siren... Angel... Lady with the

Fiery Hair… these were a few that came to mind as he smiled once again and blew the young woman a silent kiss.

He was unsure of the emotions that were filling his veins and melding with his hot blood. He assumed it was fascination or wonder, but he felt a bit nervous in his stomach, light in the head, and weak in the knees as he looked in on her. He felt an attraction toward her that he could not fully explain, but neither his mind nor his heart needed an explanation. They simply needed acceptance, and with someone as lovely and as intriguing as his sleeping angel, he knew that he would not find acceptance in someone like her.

She was perfect - flawless. She was everything that he had always dreamed the perfect woman looked like. Skin the color of the palest peach... hair as red as fire and as curly as it was long. A slender waist... ample, perked breasts... long legs and strong shoulders. She held a sophistication about her that he knew many young women lacked, and he was not up for immaturity. He was, however, very fascinated by the vixen asleep before him.

She would never be able to see him as he saw her. There was not a doubt in his mind about this. If she ever saw the scars… the damage from the fire that took much of his castle so long ago… she would never look at him again. She would call him a monster, just as the rest of the village did, albeit behind his back. She would grow fearful of him, and she would mock him for his faults and flaws, cutting a knife even deeper into his heart than was currently implanted. He simply could not bear this to happen.

Glancing once more at the sleeping maiden, he offered her a nod of his strong, if humbled, head and took a step back. Lightning crashed again through the sky, illuminating him just briefly, and when the darkness settled again, he turned from the cottage and disappeared back into the darkness of the night.

He decided then that he would not pay her another visit. She could never see him, and he could never see her again. Now, as he headed back for the hill that led to his home, he wished that she had never visited his castle at all. He wished even more that he hadn't searched out her cottage to return the mask. It occurred to him how surprised, and even shocked, she would be in the morning when she woke to find the mask awaiting her on her table. She would know without a doubt that there had been an intruder at her home – even if he hadn't been inside her bedroom with her. This would possibly frighten her, and he wondered if she would ever again be able to sleep as comfortably and soundly as she did this night.

The trek back to his castle was a brief one. He knew Foliage well, and he had made the trip to and fro many a time. Yet, when he entered inside his front door and stared around into the dark, staleness of his home, the castle had never felt so empty.

Hanging his head low, he sighed with a deep sadness, and in a bout of self-anger, he jerked his head up to the ceiling and cried out with an agony and a rage that he had never expressed with such intenseness. His scream ran long, and it echoed loudly throughout every hall and chamber of the castle and even into the blackened air outside. When this scream fell silent, he cried out once again, this time falling down to his knees in bitter self-loathing. His hands fell across his face, touching upon the scars that had sealed his doom. Running his fingers from his face to his hair, he grabbed two fistfuls of the golden locks and pulled hard, adding pain to his already crippling misery.

"Lest he who hath created his hell perish in his hell…" he whispered as the tears began to dry from his eyes. Then, with a leap, he rose to his feet and crossed the foyer to the staircase. With slow, steady movements, he began up the stairs, formulating in his thoughts what his next actions would be. His mind was hazy and in a fog, and thinking made his head only hurt more.

The stairs seemed to continue up for an eternity, but he was used to the climb and he made it to the belfry of his castle with practiced ease. There, he rushed past the old brass bell that had not rang in many, many years, and he forced his hands to brace him as he stopped abruptly at the stone encasing that prevented him from falling to his death below.

With tear-stained cheeks, he stared down at the foggy ground, barely able to see the dirt of the hill. He looked over just slightly and gazed at the village of Foliage, which was completely lost in the night and the thick of the fog surrounding it. The wind still blew with massive force, rocking against his chilled body but never once ringing the bell behind him. Had the bell decided to ring, it would have rocked up against him with enough strength that he would have been pushed from the belfry and down to the ground below, shattering every bone in his body.

This thought chilled him more than the powerful wind, and he held himself in his arms as he tried to find the cottage of the mistress with the mask. Even though he could see none of the buildings contained within Foliage, he knew now the exact location of the fair maiden's home, and he stared in that direction for the longest of time.

"What I would give," he whispered, releasing fog with his breath, "just to touch you... to hold you... to share but one dance with you."

Shaking his head, he groaned and looked down to his feet. He knew in his heart that as long as she could see his face, his dreams had no chance of edging anywhere close to reality.

"As long as she can see my face..." he repeated his thought with a striking curiousness that seemed to drift along with the flow of the wind. A light suddenly appeared in his eyes – a spark that had long been missing. With a newfound rush, he hurried back around the massive, still bell and down the eternal stairs that led from the belfry. With haste, he trampled down each step, and on the second floor, he stomped onto the landing and hurried down the hallway. Ignoring every door on his right hand side, he followed the immense hall to the very end, opening up the only door to face him head on.

Entering, he moved across the dark, cryptic room and sat down atop his unkempt bed. His strong but trembling hand reached over to the round wooden table cornered between the bed and the wall. There, he lifted a yellow scroll into his hand and pulled loose the white ribbon tied around it. He remembered well the moment he received the invitation. It had not been delivered to him in person as it should have, but it had instead been thrown up to his land from the bottom of the hill, tied to a heavy rock to ensure it would make the throw. When he found it, it was damp and dirty, and slightly torn, but it had been the first piece of lettering he had received in some time, and it made him feel rather involved and included. Ever since the night of that fateful fire, he had felt shunned, excluded from the villagers. Perhaps it had been his shame – his hatred for what the fire had done to him. Perhaps it had been the villagers' taunts and how he had become known as a monster. What it all boiled down to was he could not bear to look at himself, so how could he expect others to accept him?

He noticed it was an invitation to a ball being thrown by a family of prestigious socialites and immediately thought it was a trap – a set-up to expose the monster of the castle atop the hill.

Now, he understood the purpose of the mask the mysterious woman had dropped in his entrance foyer. It was her mask for the ball, which meant that she would be there. And if he were to attend... also masked... there was a chance that he would see her again. Perhaps... perhaps he would talk to her. Dance with her as he had earlier envisioned...

Pulling the invitation to his chest, he smiled sincerely for the first time since returning home, and he lay back against his cold, hard bed and stared up at the ceiling above.

"Ah... lady of my heart..." he thought aloud as his eyes began to drift shut. "In two days, I shall see you again. Can my heart survive that long without you?"

He stretched. A slight yawn escaped his lips. The time was late and it was best to do the one thing that would place him in the exact same spot as the woman of his dreams, he gently fell asleep. As he slept throughout the night, his smile remained etched across his strong, sturdy, scarred face.

4

The morning sunlight flooded into her room with the force of heaven's brightest star. Natalie woke to this and the sound the birds chirping outside her window, and she squinted as she tried to open her eyes for the first time this morning. She found this peculiar, as she knew that the shutters had been closed when she had gone to bed, and the sun should not have been able to get inside of her room. Then, she thought about the unpredictable current season, and she knew that it had been the wind that had intruded upon her room during the night.

She stood with a yawn, and closing her eyes again, she stretched. A chill captured her and she felt goosepimples rise across the smooth surface of her skin. Rubbing over her forearms, she opened her eyes again and moved across the room to her window.

Gazing out into the bright, early morning sunshine, she sighed with tender ease. The songs of the birds were music to her drowsy ears, and the sight of the farmers and eager merchants rushing off to begin their days was inspirational to her. Natalie placed her elbows against the window sill and smiled happily at the many familiar faces that appeared from within their waking cottages. She noticed that each of them looked in her direction as they came outside, but none of them returned the waves or smiles that she kindly offered them. The attention of the townsfolk was focused on something other than Natalie. A crowd began to form in front of her house, and she felt uncomfortable for it.

"Lord Jensen," she called out as a carriage pulled to a halt in front of her cottage. Lord Jensen, the wealthiest man in all of Foliage, was staring out of his small window, gazing at the house. "Lord Jensen, what is everyone attracted to out there?"

Lord Jensen did not reply, and neither did anyone else for that matter. In a fit of worry, Natalie tore away from the window and crossed over to her bedroom door. With a nervous hand, she opened the door and stepped out into the front room of the house. All was quiet and seemed empty inside.

"Mother?" she called loudly, looking over every inch of the cottage. "Father?"

Natalie hurried now to the front door of the house, opened it, and rushed outside to where the crowd was gathered around. At first, she stared around in bewilderment, watching the curious faces of each individual in front of her. Then, taking a step toward them, she turned around and stared at her cottage.

The cottage, itself, was fine. There was not a piece of it out of place. It was the tree beside it, however, that took precedence.

For, halfway up the tree, sprawled out over two large branches, Hiram and Roselyn slept in one another's arms. A half-empty bottle of wine rested between Hiram's bare chest and the crook of his underarm. Neither Natalie's mother nor her father were completely unclothed, but they were close enough that they were certainly causing a spectacle.

"My word..." Natalie breathed, feeling a touch faint, a touch embarrassed, and a touch amused, all at the same time.

"How did they get up there?" asked one woman to her left as she gazed at the tree in wonder. "There's no ladder... no lower branches..."

"They must have climbed onto the roof of the cottage," answered a man a few feet down from them. "It's the only way I see possible."

"You sure they didn't fly up there?" one man cackled from the back of the crowd. "They sure look like a couple of nesting birds if you ask me!"

Several people laughed at this comment, and it forced even more embarrassment over Natalie. Her worry wasn't how her parents got into the tree. Her worry was about how she would get them out of the tree. That seemed the impossible task. No solution filled her mind, and she feared that when her parents woke, they would fall out of the tree, having lost their balance from their surprise of having been up there in the first place. She could see them crashing from the branches and down to the hard grown below, breaking a leg or an arm from the impact. Then, she knew that if they fell at the wrong angle, they would fall through the roof of the cottage. The roof would cushion their fall, but it would destroy that safety shield of their house and force it into bad need of repair and renovation.

"Everybody please!" Natalie attempted to call in calm voice, but it broadcasted shaky and rough. "If we startle them, they could fall."

The villagers of Foliage decided that this was certainly information worth discussing amongst themselves, and their chattering whispers rose even higher than the tone of their earlier curious chatter.

"What on earth was in that bottle?" Natalie whispered quietly to herself as she turned her sights back to her sleeping parents, high above in the tree.

From within the branches of the tree, Roselyn began to stir. Her eyes slipped open into a tired slant. Her lips curled with the recognition of morning. Taking a deep whiff of the air, she breathed in deep the scent of the approaching spring, and this brought those curling lips to a full smile. The realization occurred to her that she had not slept as well as she had last night in quite a while, and briefly she wondered why she did not drink wine more.

A yawn began to escape her mouth, and with it, Roselyn began to rise.

"Mother, no!" Natalie froze as she watched her mother attempt to balance herself and stand, suddenly realizing that something was not right.

"Oh...!" Roselyn screeched, grabbing hold of the two branches nearest her and preventing herself from what could have been a rather messy fall. Her first feeling was a numbness of the body. The second was one of fright. It was with this moment that she realized she was, indeed, in a tree. How she came to be in this tree, she did not know. She did know that she didn't like it... not one bit.

Glancing beside her, she saw her husband Hiram, still fast asleep.

"Hiram!" she called in a hushed voice, hoping to wake him swiftly but with ease. "Hiram!"

"What... what?" the old man mumbled, stirring slightly and cradling the half-drunk bottle of wine in his hands.

"Hiram... we are up in a tree..." her voice quivered as she spoke – a rarity for Roselyn Wills.

"No... no thank you, my lady," he mumbled, shifting just enough to cause his wife's heart to stop and restart with a jolt. "I don't think I'd care for any tea this morning."

"Not tea, you old washboard! A *tree*!" Now, Roselyn was falling back into her old self, trying her best to gain control over the situation.

"Can you climb down?" Natalie yelled from the ground, noticing that the crowd behind her had fallen into a hush. They were still and awaiting the fates of two of the most beloved people in town. Natalie also noticed that none of these villagers were doing anything to try to help.

"I think this is the daughter's fault," one old man finally whispered as he stared at Natalie with grim eyes. "I heard she was on the hill last night."

Natalie swallowed deep with this, forcing her attention to turn from her distressed mother and her slumbering father and focus on the gossip brewing from the crowd behind her.

"The Hill of the Black Castle?" a woman of thirty called from the frontline. "I've never heard such nonsense. No one has been on that hill on years."

"I saw her myself!" announced a strong but very familiar voice. Natalie's eyes widened as Sarah St. John stepped to the front of the crowd. Sarah stared her nemesis dead in the eyes. "I watched her. She fled from the fountain, and I watched her climb the bloody hill. She visited the monster's castle, and now she's cursed her family."

"You snotty little rattlesnake," Natalie snapped back, refusing to take insults in her own front yard. "How dare you come to my home and insult the ground that my father worked so hard for?"

"Natalie!" Roselyn yelled timidly from her branch, but Natalie paid the woman no mind.

"You're just jealous, Natalie," Sarah continued, smiling cockily and tilting her head up to the morning sun. "You have always been jealous of me and for obvious, perfectly reasonable reasons. I'm wealthier than you. I'm more popular than you, and I am more alluring than you. But it's really not your fault at all. You can't help it if you come from a family of tree-climbing baboons!"

"If by alluring you mean a whore, then you have described yourself perfectly, Miss St. John."

The crowd released a hushed gasp at this, but it was Roselyn's voice that was heard above all others.

"Natalie!"

"Just a moment, Mother!" the young woman snapped as she turned her attention back to her parents in time to watch the branches crack and break beneath them. "Oh! Mother! Father!"

Crying out her parents' names did nothing to help save them, and they plummeted hard and heavy from the broken tree, barely missed the house, and landed with a loud thump on the ground, only feet away from Natalie. Natalie's eyes were wide, anxious. She hurried to their sides, hoping – praying – for the best. Nearly every person in the surrounding crowd rushed up to view the spectacle and to make certain that neither person had fallen dead.

Both Roselyn and Hiram were – thankfully – conscious, and Natalie exhaled an exasperated sigh of relief.

"Are you both alright?" she asked heavily, taking note of the nervousness in her voice.

"Aye, I think I am fine, my dear," Roselyn spoke through her rattled voice. "I landed on something soft… albeit your father."

"Get off of me, woman," Hiram grumbled as he rolled his wife off of him and attempting to stand. When he did, he realized a sharp pain in his leg and had to lower himself back to the ground again. "I think I broke my leg," he moaned. Then, as if he had to stop and think about it, he added, "The good leg, that is."

"Neither of your legs be good, ya ol' stiff," Roselyn cackled at her fallen husband, taking in a wee bit of humor from his pain. When he showed not a smile in return, she knew that his injury was serious. "Fine then. Up with ya now," she announced, leaning down and gathering him into her arms. With Hiram's arms around her neck, she easily supported him as he balanced on one leg. "I'll lead you into house and into the bed. The shop will have to mind itself for a few days, is all."

"Never," the old man protested as he hopped toward the front door of his cottage. "I may be limp, but I can still do my craft."

"I'll mind the shop, Father," Natalie announced, offering Hiram her hand as she aided Roselyn in guiding him inside. "I've studied under you more than enough to know the proper ways, and I can assure you that I shan't mess anything up."

"You have the spirit of your mother," Hiram grinned ever so slightly. "But you have the patience of a newborn."

"Let me run it, Father, at least 'til the weekend. Then, by the morn of Monday, you might be able to manage on your own."

Glancing to the timepiece on the front room table, he took a heavy breath and rolled his eyes. "You've got twenty minutes...no, less to be at the market and open the shop. If you cannot make it, I will open myself."

Natalie could not remember the last time that she heard her father speak so sternly, but he was in pain and had fallen limp, and the candle shop was the family's main source of income. Despite the sheer pain that shot through his nerves, he knew that the shop could not go a single day without opening. That included the weekend, Natalie knew, but she had high hopes that her mother would fill in so that she could attend the ball with the proper amount of time needed to prepare.

"Let's get you in the bed," she cooed with a smile, aiding her mother in leading him to his room. "Then, I'll get to the shop and open up for the day."

In this moment, Natalie truly felt like she had aged and become an adult. She held her smile with this thought, helping her father into his bed and covering him with a blanket. She patted his head, stroked his hair away from his eyes, and kissed him on his scruffy cheek.

"The shop is in good hands," she assured him, touching a finger to his nose before she stepped away. As she passed by her mother on her way to the door, she added, "I'll sell a whole mess of candles for you today, father. It will be wonderful."

"Just don't burn the place down," Hiram responded, winking to Roselyn.

"Father!" Shaking her head but still grinning, she stepped from the room, shutting the door behind her.

As she retreated to her room to prepare for the day, the thought of being eighteen stormed through her mind again and she realized that she was not only opening up shop for her father, but she had true responsibilities that she'd never had before. She could not remember a single time that her father had missed opening his shop, and during all of her time with him, she had learned much. Even though she was nowhere near as skilled as her father, she knew how to make a lot of the candles and she knew how to handle the customers. She was still a bit uneasy about the idea of running it without her father, but she was determined to show him that she could handle it.

For today, she chose her plainest dress, figuring melted wax would not ruin this drab fabric nearly as much as it would one of her nicer dresses that her mother had made for her. She even had a couple of store-bought dresses, but they were much too expensive and fancy for a day at work.

She considered grabbing one of her mother's aprons from the kitchen to take with her, but she remembered her father's work apron at the shop was much thicker and larger and it would protect her drab clothing from spills, although she really did not mind if the dress ruined a bit.

Sitting atop her bed, she reached down for a pair of shoes, only for her eyes to catch hold of something very strange, very peculiar – and in a way, very frightening.

Her mask – the one she'd dropped and left in the old abandoned castle – sat on her small table near the window.

"How?" she whispered, albeit to herself. "I know I dropped it. I remember the panic when I realized I'd lost it. How did it end up back here?"

Slowly, her eyes moved up from the mask to the window and froze on it.

She wondered who had found it, who had returned it, and who had invaded the privacy of her window to place it on her table.

Chills crept over her body, as only one suspect appeared in her thoughts. Even though she had seen not a soul, her mind drifted to and remained on the monster that had become so mythically linked to the castle.

"Preposterous," she said, shaking her head. "Monsters don't exist. If they did, I doubt they'd hide in an abandoned castle all their lives."

Turning away from the window and the mask, she found a ribbon to tie her hair back, quickly leaving the room thereafter.

Once more, she failed to check for a shopping list from her mother, but she wouldn't have been able to shop anyway, seeing as she would be in the candle shop all morning and afternoon. Besides, she was certain her mother had bought all of the necessities yesterday, so there would be no need for a list.

As much as she tried, the walk to the Wax shop did nothing to clear her mind. It consistently returned to the thought of the beautiful mask gifted to her by the village's so called witch.

"Somebody returned it," she said, knowing for a fact that it could not have shown up purely out of magic – no matter how good of a witch Madame Howell was.

Entering the marketplace, she looked over to the mountains where she could see the crumbling, brooding castle caped with the morning fog. It chilled her, although she was unsure as to why. She had been there; she had seen the inside. The dampness, the dust and dirt – the spiders and their massive, flowing webs. As for the so called monster that lived there, she had seen neither hide nor hair. Had a monster truly inhabited the castle, she was certain it would have come for her, attacked her, and she never would have been seen again.

The bell at the cathedral had not yet sounded, which meant she still had a few moments to spare before she was to open her father's shop. She decided that it was time to pay another friendly visit to her favorite witch.

5

Madame Howell's shop of curiosities and oddities seemed darker than usual this morning. Perhaps it was the time of day, Natalie presumed. If Madame Howell was like any of the witches she'd read about in fairy tales, then perhaps she was not an early morning person. Yet, she did not seem like the evil witches that had inhabited her childhood books. Those witches had been cruel and heartless. Despite her father's injury due to the "wine," Natalie had always found the Madame quite friendly and caring.

Yet, in this dim lighting, the curiosity shop took on a whole different feel – a darker, more intimidating feel.

"Eerie," she whispered. The shop obviously seemed closed still to the public – unopened and unmanned – and yet the door had been open for her to enter. Each step that she took was one of caution and unabridged intimidation. The "oddities" and "curiosities" all seemed much odder and more curious, and they sent ravaging chills shrieking across her flesh. Natalie had ventured to Madame Howell's shop only a few times during her young life, but she had never felt so nervous in it as she did now.

"Madame Howell?" she asked, calling out the witch's name with a trembling voice. "Madame Howell, are you here?"

There was no answer in the form of a voice, but a thump at the back of the shop made Natalie feel as if her heart had stopped. "Madame Howell?" she asked again, only this time, nothing at all made a sound in response.

On unsteady feet as if she'd just witnessed a ghost, she stepped slowly through, past the shelves and tables that held a mass of the grimmest items she'd ever seen. There were skins from animals, but the skins had no heads so she did not know what types of animals they were from. There were jars with fluids that encased other strange items, a couple of which she wondered if they had once been alive... or human.

She gulped when she came across a book with a blank cover. Touching upon the cover, she thought it too felt like skin, and once again, she wondered what kind of skin it had been. A deer? A cow or sow? A young maiden who had wondered into the shop a little too early?

"I have to stop this," she whispered in the most hushed voice she could manage. "Madame Howell has been very dear to me. There is no reason for any fearful concern."

As Natalie crept nearer to the back of the shop, she heard a rustling sound, followed by another sudden thump. The sound brought her to a halt, and it nearly stopped her heart as well.

She remembered a story she had heard passed down from

her grandmother when she was little. The story was rumored to have been a hundred years old, but she believed it to be much older than that. It had been about a demon – or perhaps an evil spirit; she couldn't remember which one – that had haunted an entire village, taking away all the children one by one. The wicked creature would appear at random places that the children would roam or inhabit, such as their bed chambers, the library, near the water of the ocean, and even the cathedral. Natalie – even to this day – was afraid of the story, and the thought that such a demon could have possibly been in the shop with her now was more than a bit terrifying.

"It's just a store," she said, trying hard to forget the tale of the demon and the thump that she'd just heard. "It's just a store and Madame Howell is my friend. There is nothing to be afraid of."

"There is always something to be afraid of, dear child," called a voice that sent a start vibrating through her skin. After a moment, Natalie calmed herself, recognizing the voice as that of Madame Howell.

"Oh," she said with a hint of exasperation, "you startled me!"

"I did not mean to frighten you, Natalie," said Madame Howell, who appeared from the back of the shop rather slowly. In the dim lighting, she looked older and more time-worn than Natalie recalled. "But I was honest. There is always something to be afraid of. Venturing to supposedly abandoned castles, for instance, could prove quite frightening for a young girl such as yourself."

"You – you know about my trip to the castle?" Natalie realized she sounded astounded, which she figured she was.

"Oh, yes," the Madame continued, "I do believe the whole village knows by now. I've heard their whispers. Everyone here whispers about everything, you know."

"Yes," the young girl agreed. "I know it all too well. People here have a tendency to stir the pot, even when there is not much in the pot to stir."

"That is the downfall of humanity – misplaced emotions and a need to dig into the lives of others." The old woman drew close to Natalie and took her hand, leading her to a set of chairs against the wall. Once seated, she peered into her eyes and smiled. "I'm glad the mask found its way back to you," she said. "You should be more cautious to not lose it in the future."

"How did you know I lost the mask?" Natalie asked, unaware that her green eyes had grown wide with wonder.

"I'm aware of many things, especially things that happen to items that leave my humble shop. You're aware of my powers, and

I'm aware of what happens to those powers when they are spread about."

"Are you telling me that you – you placed your powers in my mask?" She almost wanted to laugh, as she found herself filled with disbelief. Yet, she knew that Madame Howell had no reason to lie to her.

"It is merely enchanted, dear girl. Enchanted items always manage to find their way home."

"I'm afraid I don't understand the difference. Is it a magical mask? I mean – it is truly beautiful and a work of art, but what kind of enchantment does it hold? Will it hurt me?"

"Now, let's not be silly," Madame Howell answered. "Of course it won't hurt you. It's just meant to bring you a little luck, is all. I would say you could use a little luck, am I right?"

Thinking about her parents and – most specifically – her father who was injured and in bed, Natalie shook her head. "What kind of luck? My father did not have much luck with the wine that you sent to him and my mother. He's at home, injured and having to miss work. I don't know how much more 'luck' my family can handle."

"There is a reason," said the Madame, "for everything."

"I have to run the candle shop for him today. I'm certain I'll do fine, but I haven't but an ounce of his skill and knowledge.

His customers will be expecting the type of service that only he could provide to them."

"You underestimate yourself, Natalie. Perhaps there is a reason that you are manning Wax today instead of your dear father."

"What possible reason could that be? Like I said, I am a poor replacement for my father."

Madame Howell smiled at the young girl and took her hand into her own. "Perhaps part of your problem today is seeing yourself as a replacement instead of as his helper. Trust yourself, child. As long as you trust yourself, you should have no fears."

"But I –!" Natalie began, only to have the Madame stop her midsentence.

"No more questions or curiosities for this morning. It is time I opened my shop, and I would suggest you go and do the same. Opening late would not please your father. Am I correct?"

"Yes, Madame Howell," she responded, knowing in fact that the pleasant witch was correct. "Thank you for speaking with me. I was a bit startled by my mask showing up in my room this morning, but I'm thankful for having it returned."

"You will be stunning at the ball," the Madame said with a glimmer of pride in her eyes. "Why, you'll likely be the belle of the ball."

"I don't know about that," Natalie chided as she left Madame Howell's side and headed toward the front of the store. "If I know Sarah St. John, she will be dressed to the nines. Her family can afford such luxuries."

"And if I know you," Madame Howell said as the girl opened her shop door, "you'll be dressed to the nines as well."

Natalie smiled and stepped outside, squinting from the brightness of the morning sun. As soon as the door shut behind her, all thoughts of Madame Howell and her mysterious mask left her mind. Now, as she ambled down the cobblestone walk toward her father's candle shop, her focus fell onto Willem – his charming good looks, his sophistication and his prominence. She cared not about his fortune, even though she was well aware of how massive it was. Natalie's family had never had much money, and yet they had always been taken care of. They were survivors, and she had been taught that money made people "soft."

"If the wealthy lost all of their riches," she remembered her mother saying once, "I doubt that they would last a month on their skills and intuition."

Suddenly, she stopped in her tracks and stared blankly ahead, in deep wonderment. Everything about Willem Grillis enticed her, but was it truly what she wanted? Did she truly yearn for the life of the well-to-do, or was she content with being strong and self-reliant. Wealth was fleeting, she knew, and she worried about what would happen if Willem's family was to somehow lose their fortune. Would they be able to survive?

Her teenage mind became overrun with questions and dreadful thoughts, and deciding it best not to question the outcome of a future that has not happened yet, she shook the feelings and thoughts of peril from her mind. For now, it was Thursday, and she had her father's shop to tend to.

Just as she approached the entrance to Wax, the cathedral bells began to chime and she took pride in herself for knowing she was right on time. Although she had intended on being a bit early, she took solace in seeing that there was no one awaiting her arrival, and replacing her contemplative expression with a smile, she unlocked and opened the door.

* * * *

Three hours passed by and Natalie stood at the counter, glancing at a book she could not remember the name of, but not really reading the words. Not one soul had ventured into the shop this morning, and she was overwhelmed with boredom. Normally, the shop was bustling with business. Her father had always seemed to stay busy, and he had often needed her assistance – not just desired it. Perhaps, she thought, word had spread that her father was home and lame, and perhaps the village knew that she alone was managing the shop. Was she the turn-off to the shoppers today? Was she of no comparison to the great Hiram Wills?

Or, worse yet, had word spread of her venture to the abandoned castle and the town was afraid of her?

"Preposterous," she chided with a smirk and shook her head. "I saw no monster in that castle. If you ask me, it's a bunch of nonsense. A ghost story to scare off the children. Why, I doubt anything bad ever happened there. The family probably left for another village, leaving behind anything they hadn't needed or wanted. That makes more sense. Monsters! It's something from a fairy tale – a rather grim one at that."

She shut her book and pushed it aside on the countertop. The thought of the entire village being fooled by myth and legend made her smile and brought her a tinge of comfort. She had lived in this village her entire life, and she had never once seen a monster. Why, she had even dared to venture to the castle in question – and enter it – and still, she had seen no monster.

"If there had been a monster in that castle, I most certainly would not have lived to share my tale. Or perhaps, the monster would have held me captive in the dungeon, but that did not happen either. Foolish people with their foolish stories – the castle was certainly in disrepair, but there was not a single monster to be seen."

Even though she, herself, had seen no glimpse of the monster, Natalie suddenly began to worry again that her actions had proven to have a negative effect on her father's business. Rumors had been the downfall of more than one shop in the village over recent years, and she knew that the rumor of her and the castle would have posed some kind of blockade between Wax and many of the people themselves.

Dread stifled her as she feared the worst – wondering if her actions would cause her family to be run out of the village, or if her family would disown her over the obvious trouble she had caused.

"Silly thoughts," she whispered, "from a silly girl, most certainly. My parents would never disown me. They love me. They tell me all the time."

Another hour passed without a single customer wandering through the door. Natalie had simply sat atop her stool, motionless, not even bothering to read. She was less worried now, and growing more and more frustrated. Fortunately, she thought, it was time for her break, and she was feeling more than a bit hungry. Stepping from her stool, she left the counter, her book, and the untouched variety of candles behind her and stepped toward the front door.

Wandering outside, the afternoon sun was high above her and temporarily distorted her vision. She turned away from its brightness long enough to lock up the shop, and when she turned back, she could feel her heart sink deep into her chest.

"Would you care for a cup of tea?" Sarah St. John asked with an untrustworthy smile engulfing her face. "My treat, of course."

"I was just going to wander down to the deli for a bite to eat," Natalie replied, startled by her nemesis's sudden presence but still able to find her words.

"Nonsense," the girl said. "I heard you were managing your father's shop today, and I decided you could use a break. Besides, seeing as your family was not able to provide you with a proper celebration for your birthday, I decided I should treat you to tea and a pastry. I, myself, will just have tea, of course. After all, I don't want to have to literally squeeze into my dress on Saturday. It should flow around my natural curves."

Natalie had a snide reply ready to voice, but she decided against it. Her mother surely would have scolded her if she knew she was even considering lowering herself to Sarah's level of rudeness.

Instead, she agreed to the cup of tea, and despite the feeling of hunger that ached in her stomach, she turned down the idea of a pastry. "I better skip on the pastry. I'd hate to have to have my seams let out at the last minute."

"Smart girl," Sarah replied. "One cannot be too safe before the ball of the year, after all."

6

They sat at a wooden table with white linen outside of the village's only café. Neither Natalie nor Sarah had spoken a word to one another since arriving, and each had ordered a simple cup of earl gray. It was halfway through their cup of tea that Sarah spoke, and just the sound of her voice made Natalie's ears burn.

"So, do you think he'll be there – at the ball?"

"Who?" Natalie asked at the blunt, random question.

"The monster, of course." the girl smiled and sipped her tea.

Natalie cringed at the response and lowered her eyes to the table. She had been waiting for Sarah to bring up her visit to the castle, and a part of her wondered what had taken so long.

"I saw no monster in that castle," she said finally, barely breathing the words – much less fully speaking them.

"It must have been hiding then, because everyone knows that a monster of a man lurks within those dire, crumbling walls."

"All that I saw within those walls," continued Natalie, "was furniture covered in sheets, dusty portraits on the walls, and enough cobwebs to open a silk shop."

"So, now we know that the monster does not have a maid.

Surely there was some sign of him."

The only sign of anything eerier than the state of the castle, Natalie knew, was the fact that her mask had somehow been returned to her, yet that was not something she wished to divulge with Sarah. It would have turned into another mess of rumors and mistruths, and that was the very last thing her family needed at the moment.

"Well," Sarah said after a moment of disturbing silence, "either way it goes, it will definitely be the ball of the year. I hear the Grillis's have hired musicians used by the King himself to perform, and the food is to be provided by a brilliant chef out of London. By the way, who's doing your hair?"

"My hair?" Natalie asked, and the tone of her voice admitted that this was the first time she'd thought of her locks.

"Of course your hair, silly. Father has brought in a stylist from Paris to do mine. He insists that my hair and my dress resemble that same cultural statement. Father says nothing is too good for me, his little princess."

Sarah's use of the word princess filled Natalie's mouth with a bitter taste. She could almost imagine her arriving to the ball with a tiara on her head.

"I suppose my mother will fix my hair," she finally answered. "Mother is very talented, after all. She made my dress for me as a surprise for my birthday."

"Well now," chided Sarah with a mischievous grin, "isn't that quaint?"

A great part of her wanted to slap Sarah – to take what remained of her cooling tea and splash her in the face with it – but Natalie retained her composure and sipped the tea instead. She smiled, looked away toward the afternoon sun, and shifted in her seat.

"It is quaint," she responded, making eye contact once more with her frenemy. "After all, the hard work and time that she put into my gown speaks volumes for the love that she has for me. You see, Sarah, my family does not have much money, but what we lack in wealth, we make up for in heart."

At first, Sarah had no response, which filled Natalie's bones with joy. Then, as if intentionally turning the tables on her, the girl turned the subject to another delicate notion. "Speaking of heart," she began as she locked into eye contact, "I think I have a pretty fair chance at wooing Willem's. I've not only been perfecting my waltz, but I've been practicing every move I'll make and every word I will speak. I do hope the other girls are attending the ball just for fun, because I have every intention of becoming the future Lady of Grilles Manor."

Although the idea of Sarah winning Willem's heart made

Natalie sick to her stomach, she knew that the girl had a much better chance at it than she. While as her parents believed her to be the most beautiful girl in the village, compared to Sarah's wealth, fine clothing and jewelry, she seemed rather plain.

"I am just excited to be invited at all," she replied. "I've been excluded from balls and events so often that I was certain Willem would have overlooked me." Then, just to dig into Sarah, she added, "I guess he thought of me after all."

"Of course he thought of you," Sarah remarked. "Why, he remembered every girl in the village. Even Maple Stines received an invitation."

This was not the response that Natalie had hoped for, as Maple Stines was the plumpest, plainest girl in the village. While Maple had the spirit and personality of a saint, she truly was hard on the eyes.

"Maple deserves to have a nice time," she said, placing her demeaning thoughts of Maple aside. "She's a good girl with a lot of joy to give to the world. I think she'll make a great addition to the ball."

Sarah sipped her tea and said nothing. Natalie wondered if she was finally getting to her. Were her kind and compassionate words finally surpassing Sarah's derogatory comments? She smiled politely and took the last sip of her now-cold tea.

"Maple is a heifer," Sarah said, regaining the wicked smile that she carried so well, "but I suppose your right. Perhaps this will be her one and only opportunity to find a man who can tolerate such a person, and why should anyone stand in the way of that? After all, I suppose we all dream of being happy someday. I just hope that whoever makes Maple happy is also happy with her."

"Maple is a good person. She has always been generous with her time, and she has helped more people in this village than either of us can claim to have done. She'll make a man very happy one day, I'm certain of it."

Natalie was growing more than a bit irritated with the direction that the conversation had taken. She stifled herself and fell silent, patiently awaiting Sarah's next snide comment. For the first time, the girl impressed her by saying nothing. This was how Natalie preferred her – silent and hopefully considering her own behavior and words. Yet, she knew Sarah better than that. They had been "friends" for their entire lives, and Sarah neither considered her own actions nor stayed silent for very long.

As Sarah opened her mouth, Natalie knew that she was above to be proven correct.

"Nobody seems to be visiting your father's shop today," she began, and Natalie sighed deep within herself. "I've been by it five times this morning, I'm sure. What say you call it a day and the two of us spend the rest of the afternoon shopping? I know you don't have many funds to spend on yourself, so it will be my treat. Consider it a belated birthday present."

Sarah was the only girl Natalie knew that could mix crassness with a kind gesture and do it so well.

"That's very kind of you," she said, nearly choking on the words, "but I made a promise to my father and it would be wrong of me to break that. Maybe some other time though?"

"Of course," Sarah said as she stood from her chair. "I would walk you back to the shop, but I feel like I should be heading on. I'm certain you understand."

"Of course."

Without another word, the two girls parted ways – Sarah toward her spending expedition, and Natalie, still seated in her chair at the table. She felt that Sarah had been correct. What was the point in her clamoring back to the shop when there had not been a single customer all day? Yet, she too had been correct in that it would have been wrong of her to have broken her promise to her father. Besides that, there was nothing she desired less than having to endure the company of Sarah St. John for a moment longer than necessary.

Finally, she stood with a stretch, releasing a slight yawn as she did. The tea had relaxed her, and it had made her somewhat sleepy. Yet, her day was only half complete, and as she neared the Wax shop, she knew this second half of the day was going to drag on for a while. When the shop came in to view, there was not one waiting customer outside.

Reaching for her key, she went to unlock the door, only to find it already open. Cautiously, she stepped inside to find her father at the counter and a mass of customers demanding his attention.

"Natalie," he chimed upon seeing her, "it's about time you returned. Help Mrs. Keaton chose the right scent for the candles for her daughter's wedding next month."

Amazed, Natalie took a moment to respond, as she could not help but wonder where all of the customers had come from and how her father had made his way into the shop. Still, she chose not to question any of it and instead made her way to Mrs. Keaton, who was admiring Hiram's latest candle colors.

"Mrs. Keaton, is there any theme in general for the wedding?" She smiled toward her father as she asked her question, but Hiram was much too busy to have noticed. Still, it relaxed her to know that she had not killed off his business after all.

7

As it turned out, Hiram's leg had not been broken as a result of his fall. He had told Natalie – once things calmed down at the shop – that Roselyn had insisted it had all been in his head. After Natalie had ventured to the store to open it for the day, Roselyn had let Hiram nap, but once he had awoken, she'd made him try to stand.

"I near 'bout broke my whole body," he told his daughter while explaining his story. "She wanted me to apply pressure to the leg, and I just collapsed."

"But you seem find now," Natalie said, noting that he was walking around even better than before. "What happened?"

"My hip – it was out of place."

"Did you pop it back in yourself?" she questioned, cringing from the thought of the pain he must have suffered.

"Oh, no! I didn't dare. You know how I am. I'm not much into pain." Then, after a pause, he added, "Your mother did it for me."

Natalie had to chuckle as she stepped outside, waiting for her father as he locked up the shop for the evening.

"Your mother is a spunky lass," the middle-aged man

added. "If not for her, I'd still be laid up in the bed."

"Well, I'm glad you've recovered, Father," Natalie said with a smile and a hug. "I still wonder how you happened into that tree."

"I wonder the same, my child. A bit too much wine, I suppose. Regardless, I feel fine now and was glad to be able to come in to work. Half the town was at the house after I fell, so I figured you must have had a pretty easy morning."

Natalie nodded and smiled, content now that there was an explanation to the day's slowness at the shop that did not involve her being the one on duty.

"Sarah St. John took me for tea at break," she said, unsure of why she did so. Her father knew of her dislike for Sarah.

"You went? I must say, I'm impressed."

"Impressed?" she questioned. She thought for certain he would have ridiculed her.

"It takes a strong person to break bread with one's enemy," he continued. "I know you and Sarah have had a rocky history, but you proved yourself strong by taking her up on her offer. What did you two discuss?"

"Oh, the usual."

"Ah, so Sarah spent the time talking about Sarah, did she? It seems to be her favorite subject."

"She tried so hard to make herself seem superior to me and to everyone else, Father. At times… it seemed to work."

"Some people may have more riches than you, but you have one of the biggest hearts of anyone I know and that is something that can never be taken away from you."

As Hiram hugged his daughter, Natalie thought to herself how fortunate she was to have such a compassionate, thoughtful father. He seemed to always know the right things to say, and better yet, he seemed to always mean them.

"Thank you, Father," Natalie whispered, enjoying the embrace.

"I love you, my daughter," he said warmly. "You are the light of my life."

As their hug broke, Natalie looked into her father's caring eyes and smiled. However, her moment of bliss would not last, as the sound of people clamoring behind them brought a start to both her and her father.

"Mr. Wills," they heard a voice exclaim, and as they turned around, they saw a man – John Brickman – approaching them with swiftness. "Mr. Wills, your shop – it's caught ablaze!"

Sure enough, they could see the smoke. Wax was burning from within, filling the air outside with clouds of gray and black. Hiram left his daughter's side, hurrying toward his shop with fear filling his bones.

"Father, wait!" Natalie cried as she chased after him, but for a man who had just suffered a great fall, he moved with speed and ease. "Father!"

Arms wrapped around her, restraining her. She caught a glimpse of John's face as he held her back, refusing to let her enter into the inferno.

"It's too dangerous!" he shouted, but she fought him nonetheless. "There is too much smoke!"

"Let go of me!" she cried, stomping on his foot to loosen his grip. Once freed, she charged toward the shop, only to stop dead in her tracks.

The roof over the entrance crashed down to the ground, right before her eyes. She could see flames trickling out from the wall behind it, catching the sign out front on fire. The door, which was still open, was engulfed in the inferno, and through the flames, she could see no trace of her father.

Natalie began to charge forward, only to have John once more hold her back.

She could hear people all around her calling her father's name – shouting it with intensity, but there was no response from Hiram. What had happened, she wondered through her panic. Had there been candles lit inside? Hadn't they extinguished them all when they closed up shop? Why was her father not answering?

"It's not safe for anyone to go in there," John whispered into her ear, but she paid him no mind. Fighting back tears, she stared up at the Wax signage, watching the letters burn away more quickly than she could have imagined. She began to cough from the smoke that flooded around her, speeding up and off into the sky, and suddenly, she could hear nothing – as if she had fallen deaf. Only a loud buzzing sound filled her head and everything around her became blurry and distorted. Her knees grew weak; her stomach twisted and turned with the force of an onslaught of nausea.

She felt she would faint, and suddenly, she was thankful that the farmer was holding on to her. Otherwise, she would have literally crumpled to the ground.

"The blaze is too strong," John said, but she could not hear him. She could only feel herself being pulled away. "I have to get you away from here."

Somewhere – perhaps in the distance or perhaps right in front of her – she could hear something faint and faded. Only one sound – a crying sound, or more of a scream – deathly and sorrowful. She recognized the voice that it was wrenched from – it was her father's voice, and he was in pain. Then, as quickly as she heard it, it was gone.

* * * *

It was as if her heart had stopped or her soul had left her body. Through the chaos and clamoring, everything around her seemed to come to a stop. She felt empty – alone. Although John was right there with her, even he seemed to disappear. She did not need to hear. She did not need to see or feel. She knew. Without anyone telling her, she knew.

At this moment, the three men that had entered the shop on their mission of rescue began to reemerge, and with them, they carried a limp, motionless and badly burned body. Even through the smoke and the charring of the skin, she could see him and she knew who he was. She knew what had happened. She knew that on this day that he had called her the light of his life, her father had lost that life. Hiram Wills was dead.

"No…" she said in a whisper at first, as if refusing to believe any of what she saw. It made perfect sense to her that her eyes were playing tricks on her, but her heart knew better. It knew the truth. Then, her whisper turned to a roar – a loud and deafening scream that shook John away from her. "No!"

As she charged toward the men, she could feel John reach for her again, but she slipped through his grip and pushed past the ever-growing crowd of spectators and of individuals still attempting to contain or put out the fire.

In the instant that the three men laid the body on the ground, Natalie was upon them. She knelt to her father's side, caressing his blackened cheek, unable to hold the tears away any longer. They flooded out of her like a storm flooding the plains. Several people tried to pull her away, but she refused. She could hear them speak to her – possibly trying to comfort her – but she could not make out their words. All that she knew was that her father was dead, and that he, too, had been the light of her life.

Once again, as everything around her became a blur, she could feel the urge to pass out – to faint, and this time, she could not prevent it.

8

Stillness encompassed the Wills' home on this night in a way that nothing else ever had. The windows were closed throughout – each blackened with dark fabric to keep away any sign of the outside world. The door was locked and the fireplace was empty, as a fire was the last thing that Roselyn or Natalie needed in their lives right now.

There was one flame, however – a flicker on a candle created by Hiram and given to his wife as a gift. It smelled of lavender and seemed to fill the entire room with its scent. It was almost as if Hiram was there, but he was not, and there was no pretending otherwise. Hiram had died and his wife and daughter were left to face their lives now without him.

Roselyn sat in a rocking chair facing a wall. She held two needles with yarn in one hand and a partially finished doily in the other, but she was not knitting. She was very still, and had she not blinked every so often, one would have wondered if she too had died, or if she had been frozen away in time.

Natalie watched her from a spot on the floor. She sat with her knees pulled up and her arms wrapped around them. Her cheeks were still stained from the tears that had gushed down for the last several hours. Yet, she could cry no more. Not now. She had cried so much that it had physically exhausted her, and she thought that if she were to cry again, it would be the end of her.

There was silence for a while. It was thick and – if Natalie could have smelled it - it would have reeked. Natalie knew that she was in shock; that was the cause for her loss of words. Her mother, she thought, must have been going through so much worse.

"I cooked supper," she heard her mother whisper, but the woman did not move and so Natalie wondered if she had actually heard her or if she had imagined it. Then, Roselyn spoke again. "It's cold by now, but we should eat. We should eat and everything will be okay."

Then, turning in her chair, she faced her daughter with tears in her eyes. "Right, Natalie? Then we'll be okay?"

Natalie did not know how to respond. While as she had just turned eighteen, she was still a child inside, and it broke her heart to see her mother in this saddened state. She opened her mouth and tried to answer, but no words could be found. Instead, she forced herself to her feet, and with nervous shakiness, she approached Roselyn, knelt down beside her, and took her into her arms.

For long moments, the two cried into each other's embrace, sobbing heavily between every gasp and breath. Then, softly, Natalie pulled away and wiped her eyes. She smiled at Roselyn and took her hand.

"Mother," she began, finally finding her voice, "Father would not like seeing us like this. He would want for us to be strong, and he would want for us to smile."

"You, dear girl," Roselyn said in a whispering breath, "have your father's wisdom."

This nearly made Natalie cry again but she fought the feeling away. She knew she had to be strong for her mother, and for herself. She would have to help Roselyn prepare for Hiram's funeral service, and surely, she would have to find work, as the Wax store was no more. It had been unsalvageable, and the fire claimed everything within.

"I will help all I can, Mother," she told Roselyn, forcing a smile and gazing into the woman's grief-stricken eyes. "I will clean houses. I can sew and bake. I will find work and we will be alright."

"Sweet child, do not worry yourself with that right now. We will survive; we always have." Roselyn fell silent for a moment, and Natalie watched in awe as the woman smiled. "Tomorrow will be a rather long day, I'm afraid. Father Harris will be coming over. He has your father's body at the church currently. I know it is customary to have the body rest at home until its burial, but under the circumstances of how Hiram passed, Father

Harris insisted we let him tend to him."

"When do you imagine we will bury him?"

"Sunday," the woman responded, displaying a bit of life in her voice. "It is the Lord's day, after all. Your father would have preferred that."

"And Father Harris will oversee everything?"

"The wonderful man has offered to handle everything. I have no concerns there. Tomorrow will be about us, handling the rest of the village."

"What do you mean?" she asked with a confused tone.

"We will have visitors likely from dawn until dark, and if we should venture out, everyone will ask how we are and if we need anything. And we'll have to be strong and not break down at the mention of your father's name. We'll have to smile kindly when people share with us their fond memories of him. After all, Natalie, we're not the only ones mourning your father right now. A lot of people cared for him, and a lot of people are going to miss him."

Natalie smiled and nodded her head. Heartbroken as she was, she knew that her mother was right and that they would have to remain strong – for everyone else, and for themselves.

"And, by God, my child, there will be food. Everyone will bring us food. It's customary when a family loses an important member."

"I know that we will have to dress in black for a while, Mother. How long will that period last?"

"For you, it will last tomorrow, and then it will last again from Sunday for seven days."

Curiously, Natalie questioned her mother's response. "But what about Saturday?"

"Saturday, you have a ball to attend, my dear, and a beautiful dress to wear to it. Black would not be appropriate."

"Mother!" she exclaimed, taken aback by the mention of the ball. She admitted to herself that she had forgotten all about it throughout today's devastation, and the idea of attending it now did not appeal to her at all. "I couldn't possibly. It'd be selfish and dishonorable of me to attend an event like that on the foothills of my father's death. He'd be devastated! He'd be saddened! He'd be …"

"He'd be angry and hurt if you chose not to go," continued Roselyn, cutting her off. "He wanted this for you so much. Honor your father by making him proud and attending that ball. He loved you so much. He only wanted for your happiness, and both of us believed that you would find happiness at this ball."

Although the notion made her feel warm and loved, she truly was uncertain that it was the appropriate thing for her to do under the circumstances. While she had been dreaming of attending this ball and perhaps sharing a dance with Willem Grillis, her father had just died a terrible death and she and her mother were left to fend for themselves and to mourn the sudden loss. She wanted to tell her mother how preposterous the idea was, but Roselyn was smiling, and that smile melted young Natalie.

She neither agreed nor disagreed, and instead, she hugged her mother again.

"Let me prepare a bite for us to eat, Mother," she said as the hug broke. "I know neither of us are very hungry, but if we must eat, we must. This has been a long day. I'd prefer it if you tried to relax and enjoy your knitting."

"Such a wise person you've become," Roselyn responded hoarsely. "When did my little girl grow up on me?"

Natalie smiled, but she did not respond. She took her mother's hand for just a moment before releasing it and moving into the kitchen. There was nothing less that she wanted than to eat, and although she knew her mother likely felt the same, she knew they needed some kind of nourishment in their stomachs.

She gazed at the spread her mother had prepared. It looked delicious – and it had obviously been prepared for three people – but it was heavier than she knew her stomach would be able to handle. She and her mother needed something lighter tonight.

After a moment of staring blankly around the room, she took the loaf of bread she'd purchased from the market earlier in the week and sliced off two nice pieces. Then, she took the marmalade that her mother had bought the week before and spread a thin helping over each piece of the bread. After plating them, she returned to Roselyn in the front room and handed her a piece.

"Eat this," she said, moving across the room to her chair. "It'll make both of us feel better."

Roselyn did as she was told and Natalie followed by example. Within moments, both daughter and mother had finished their helping. A moment of silence followed. It was a somewhat uncomfortable silence, although Natalie could not reason why. Perhaps it was the fact that after a meal, her father would have always been the one to ignite conversation amongst the family. Now, without their patriarch, both she and Roselyn seemed lost for words.

A yawn slipped from Natalie's lips and Roselyn glanced toward her.

"If you're sleepy, child, then you should sleep. I will be fine."

"I would hate to leave you here alone, Mother," Natalie answered, but she could not fight the fact that Roselyn was right. She was more than sleepy – she was exhausted. The fire and loss of her father had been a mental, physical and emotional strain on her, and she needed rest.

"Sleep," Roselyn commanded in a gentle tone. "Tomorrow will come whether we rest or not, but we'll both be able to handle it better with a bit of shuteye."

She couldn't argue any further. Standing once more, Natalie crossed to her mother and gave her a final hug for the night. She whispered that she loved her and kissed her on the forehead, offering a sweet – yet strong – smile as she retreated to her bedroom.

In her room, she changed into her sleeping gown and slid beneath her covers. In the darkness, she shut her eyes and prayed to drift off to sleep quickly, but her prayer seemed unanswered. Her mind was plagued by images of the fire and thoughts of her father. She tossed and she turned, reliving in her mind the last moments that she had spent with Hiram, and worse, the image of her father being brought out of the burning candle shop, dead.

She felt that she was to blame. She felt that she could have stopped him from charging into the building, or that she should have checked one last time to make certain that all candles had been extinguished. Had she held her father's hug just a moment longer, would that have kept him from reaching the building in time to enter it? Had she sealed his death herself?

She opened her eyes as she heard the sounds of her mother entering into her own bedroom and shutting the door behind her. She hoped that Roselyn would be able to rest. Natalie could not imagine what it would be like for her. Roselyn and Hiram had always shared a bed. She knew that it would be a strain on her mother spending the night alone.

Yet, she also knew that Roselyn needed to mourn, and Natalie had no right to stand in the way of that. Whereas Natalie had lost her father, Roselyn had lost her husband, and she knew that the grief in that was deeper than she could imagine.

As her eyes adjusted to the darkness, she looked at the small wooden table beside her bed and stared at the mask Madame Howell had given her. It seemed to look back at her. It tormented her with the ideas of the ball only a day and a half away. It tortured her with the thought that her father would not get to see her in her outfit, and he would not get to hug her or wish her well. It made her quiver and she forced herself to look away.

Towards her ceiling, she stared again into darkness, yet the shadows seemed to move and play tricks on her eyes. It was the exhaustion, she decided, that was toying with her mind, and so she shut her eyes in yet another attempt to fall asleep. This time, she was more successful, and her mind finally let her rest.

9

Although she had slept, morning seemed to arrive much too early for Natalie. In fact, she felt anything but rested, as her body was sore and her brain felt somehow muted and incredibly clouded. Perhaps, she thought, the events of yesterday had only been a dream, but the emptiness in her heart reminded her that they had, indeed, been real. Her father was dead, her mother was single, and Natalie was at the halfway point of becoming an orphan.

She stood and stretched, and despite wanting nothing more than to retreat back beneath the safety of her covers, she tended to her morning rituals. Once she was clean, fresh and dressed, she joined her mother in the kitchen to find her breakfast awaiting her at the table.

"Eggs and ham?" Roselyn asked in a semi-upbeat tone, as if nothing at all had changed in their lives. "We did not eat much at all last night, so I figured you might be famished.

Natalie sat at the table and took a small bite of the eggs. She was not famished, but she hated to disappoint her mother. "Delicious," she remarked, and the more that she ate, the hungrier she realized she was. Before long, her plate was clear of food and she stood, carrying the empty dish over to the counter. "What can I do today to help?"

"Well, you can start by getting out of the house and getting some fresh air," Roselyn said in a spunky tone, complete with a smile. "Father Harris will be coming by soon to discuss the arrangements, and I would prefer it if you were out and about instead of here, dealing with the depressing details."

"I don't think you should have to do this alone," Natalie combated.

"I don't think that's your choice," her mother replied. "Either way, I won't be dealing with it alone. Father Harris will help me on any decision that must be made, so I'll be in good hands."

Once again, Natalie found that it was pointless to argue. Still, she did not know what she would do. It felt a bit odd to her to not be heading to her father's shop. She had often helped out, especially on Fridays, but now, there would be no point in it.

Yet, there was this piece of her that yearned to pay it a visit. Perhaps – just perhaps – she would be able to slip inside, if for no other reason than a bit of closure.

* * * *

Although the village's center of commerce was bustling, to

Natalie, it felt very empty. In the air, she swore that she could still smell with every inhale the smoke of the fire, yet she seemed to be the only one who noticed the aroma.

Her mother had warned her last night that people in the village would possibly stop her to check on her and ask her how she was doing in the aftermath of her father's death, and it honestly surprised her that, as of yet, not one person had stopped to greet her. Many had nodded as they hurried from shop to shop, and a few had smiled politely, albeit not breaking from the random conversations they were having with others as they strolled about. Yet, at least so far, no one had truly seemed to notice her.

Coming to a standstill, she stared ahead, seeing the charred remains of her father's shop. While the structure was still standing, the damage to it was blatantly obvious. There were pails and buckets sitting outside from where people had worked to extinguish the fire, and only part of the "x" remained on the charred, fallen sign. The entrance to the building was roped off to the public, for the door was of no use. In fact, there was not much of a door remaining at all.

Taking a deep breath, she stepped up to the entrance, and as she moved through it, her body began to feel numb.

A flood of memories swarmed over her. She could remember standing at the remains of the counter as a little girl, although then it had been new and pristine. Her father had always placed a small stepladder behind the counter for her to climb atop, so that she could see above the countertop and chat with the customers as they came in.

A tear fell from Natalie's eye with the memory, but she wiped it away. She refused to cry right now.

The wax room where she and her father had made candles was at the back of the building, but there was still steamy smoke trickling out of it. Curiously, she wanted to look in it and see if anything had remained.

"You know, you really shouldn't be in here," called a voice from behind her, startling a gasp from her.

Turning around, she saw Widow Rosamond, whose husband had passed away when Natalie was five.

"Mrs. Rosamond, you startled me."

"My apologies, dear child, but I saw you slip in here and this place is much too dangerous to be investigated right now. Why, it could collapse down on you at any moment." Although her words were firm, she said them with the most pleasant of smiles.

"I'm sorry. I just – I had to see."

"To make sure it was real?"

Natalie nodded her head. Her heart told her that Widow Rosamond fully understood her intentions.

"I am sorry to hear about your father, Natalie, but this is not a good place for you to mourn. Perhaps you'll join me for a cup of tea? I've had experience in losing people I love. Maybe I can be of some help."

"I appreciate the sentiment, Mrs. Rosamond, but I do not believe I'm quite ready to talk about it yet." Natalie felt her eyes well up with tears again, but she managed to fight them away.

"The offer will stand – whenever you are ready." The old lady smiled again and took Natalie's hand, leading her out of the Wax Shoppe. "Losing someone you love is hard, but you should know that they are never gone completely."

"What do you mean?"

"Just like with my sweet husband, your father will always watch over you. Remember that when you miss him – that he is always there."

Widow Rosamond held Natalie's hands for just a moment longer and gazed at her with a smile. Then, letting the girl's hands slip away, she turned and departed, disappearing into the growing crowd of shoppers and merchants on the street.

Although she still wanted to cry, Natalie chose not to and took a deep breath instead. Letting the air slowly escape her lungs, she brought her focus back on tomorrow night's ball and the fact that her father would want her to enjoy it.

"I did not expect to see you out and about today," she heard a voice call, once again startling her. Turning around, she faced Sarah St. John. "I guess there's no time to mourn with a grand ball tomorrow night."

"I am still mourning," Natalie replied with a slight grimace. "Mother insisted I get out of the house today so that she could plan Father's services with the priest."

"Well, you are dressed in black, so I can see you're following tradition. Will you be wearing black to the ball tomorrow as well? It's not really the color I'd choose, but – "

"I'll be wearing the dress my mother made for me. She insists."

"You know, the offer is still on the table. I'd be happy to take you to have your hair done appropriately."

Natalie knew that Sarah was being kind – in her own little way – but it was infuriating to her.

"Sarah, this is not a good time for me. I have some errands to do, and then I need to rush home to see how Mother and the good father are handling arrangements."

It was a lie that she had errands to do. Mother had sent her out to relax, but Sarah was not bringing relaxation. She was making her more stressed, whether the upper-crust girl realized it or not.

"Okay, well, I tried to help. I guess I failed," Sarah snipped, turning her back to Natalie and walking off. Natalie could feel the burn of her motions as she walked away, but she did not care. She had more important things on her mind than dealing with an arrogant girl's mediocre attempt at kindness.

A middle-aged couple that Natalie barely recognized approached her. When she first saw them, they were smiling. Now, the closer they got to her, the more their smiles turned to frowns.

"Oh, my," the gentleman said, lowering his head, "we are both so sorry to hear about Hiram. He was such a good man."

"You must be devastated," the woman said, touching Natalie on the chin – something she hated. "Absolutely devastated."

"We are here for you if you need us," the man continued. "Just say the word."

"Anything at all," said the woman, and they departed without another word.

There were three more encounters like this, and Natalie felt as if she hadn't walked but a few steps between each one. More frowning faces; more terms of endearment and condolence.

"How is your dear mother holding up?" Randall Bishop asked her. He was known for being the town letch. "You tell Roselyn that if she needs a shoulder to cry on, mine is more than available."

"How is your wife?" she asked him. Randall's reputation was widely the source of gossip, and his wife had been one of her father's clients.

"Mourning your father's death, assuredly. No one could fill my wife's waxing needs like your dear papa could."

"Well," Natalie said as politely as she could, "Mother is mourning his death also, and I believe she has a meeting with the priest. His shoulder must be the holiest of all to cry on, wouldn't you say?"

Randall blushed and looked anywhere but in Natalie's eyes. "I see she is in good hands. That is wonderful. Please, though – send my regards," he said as he hurried away.

"I can't take this anymore," she said, not caring if anyone heard. "Mother was right. Everyone knows about Father. I don't need this right now. I need peace. I need solitude."

When she finally walked again, it was more than just a walk. It was a hurried stride through frustrated huffs. She pushed her way through the market shoppers, ignored every single person that spoke her name, and made eye contact with no one. She walked so swiftly and with unknown purpose that she truly did not know where she was walking to. Eventually, the town faded away behind her, but she neither realized this nor cared. She did not stop moving until she had reached a ground only vaguely familiar – one that she had only been to once. When she stopped, she was at the castle of the so-called beast.

10

"A beast, they call him," she chided as she walked along the stone-lined wall that lead the way to his castle entrance. "A beast, my foot. They are the beasts – always whispering and talking behind the backs of those who have never done a thing to them. Always judging and pushing and clamoring for more information and more details and more gossip and rumors!"

She had to stop walking, as her frustration was getting the better of her and she was finding it hard to breathe. Still, even though she no longer walked, she continued to vent her thoughts and scarred emotions.

"There is no peace. There is no rest. They will not be satisfied until they have drained everything I am from my very bones. My father is freshly departed, and still they speak away, either to me or as if I wasn't even there. How dare they? How dare people have to audacity to be so cruel, so heartless?"

Again, she moved, ever closer to the castle's entrance.

"How dare they ask me to tell them all about my feelings? How dare they try to befriend me when they have otherwise ridiculed me? How dare they treat me like a child and like they are the gloves that can hold me and force me to part with the feelings that are sweeping throughout my insides?"

Atop the front steps of the castle's grand entrance, she stopped, resting her hand on a column that was near destruction.

"They have me so frustrated – so angry! I could... I could just scream!"

Yet, she did not scream. Instead, Natalie felt heat and tension rise through her body, and in the quickest moment, the world around her grew hazy and blurred. Then, quiet suddenly, everything went dark as she tumbled down to the hard stone floor of the entrance porch.

* * * *

There was calmness, distinct and uninterrupted. As her eyes opened, the world was still a blur, but the world had also somehow changed. She was no longer on the castle's cold and rigid porch. Instead, she was in a room, warm and secured. Was it her bedroom, she wondered. Had everything been a dream, or had someone rescued her and returned her to her home?

Her mother was surely worried of her condition and she wanted to call out to her, but Natalie was weak – too weak to even speak. She tried to remember what had happened, and she could remember her frustration and the tension that had built within her, but nothing more. It was all very confusing to her. How would anyone have known where to find her to begin with? She had departed the village. She had roamed to a place that most were fearful to venture. Who could have found her?

As her blurry vision began to clear, she suddenly realized a very peculiar and somewhat frightening fact. She was not at home in her bedroom.

In fact, her surroundings were so unfamiliar to her that she began to grow frightened. The bed was more than twice the size of her own. The room, twice as large. The sheets that her body lay between were a much higher grade fabric than what her mother and father could have afforded. The furniture was old, but classy and stylish. There was even a canopy that hung around the bed, billowing from the breeze of an open window.

Sitting up, she tried to stand but immediately felt dizzy again. After giving herself a moment to recover, she rose up from the bed and looked toward the open window. Natalie moved to it slowly, grasped hold of the sill, and stared out at the dead courtyard of what could only be the beast's castle.

"How?" she whispered, still wishing she remembered more of her arrival here. "Who brought me inside?"

Turning from the window, she gazed again at her surroundings. Although she could touch and feel the items in the room, it all felt very surreal, as if she was locked in a dream. Perhaps, she thought, that was it. Perhaps she was in a dream.

Pinching herself, she knew that she was very much awake. This was no dream. She was standing in a bedroom inside the monster's castle.

"How long have I been in slumber?" she wondered, looking at the bed and then at the large, golden framed mirror that hung on the wall beside it. "This is very peculiar, and I must return home."

Through the mirror image, she checked herself, ensuring that she was still dressed in the clothing that she had arrived in. The black of her dress was stark and appropriate, considering her current state of mourning. Her red hair was somewhat tangled from the bed, but she smoothed it over to where it seemed merely windblown. Her face was pale – presumably from her fainting spell – and so she pinched her cheeks in an effort to return some color to them.

"I should probably be a bit more frightened than I actually am," she admitted, turning away from the mirror and facing the bedroom door. "Well, I've had enough frights for one lifetime."

Edging close to the door, she stared at it with distinct curiosity. Her hand trembled as she reached for it, and as she clutched its cold knob, she forced a swallow that had otherwise been caught in her throat. Turning the knob, she pulled the door open just a few inches, startled by the sudden sound of its creaking.

"It's just a door… inside a castle… There is nothing to be afraid of here."

Pulling the door open wide, she listened as the creaking dissipated and stared out into the darkness of a hallway. Touching upon the door frame, she felt the thick stickiness of a long abandoned cobweb and she cringed. As she stepped into the hall, her foot bumped against something – making it move on the floor, startling her. In her surprise, she jumped back a bit and skipped both a breath and a heartbeat. She looked at the ground and the object that had caused her fright. Bending downward to inspect it, she discovered that the object was a plate that was filled with food. Her stomach gurgled its approval at the sight of it, but Natalie was not quite as easily assured.

Touching upon the meat on the plate, she found it to be warm.

"I don't trust it," she whispered, taking another step back. "I won't take even a nibble." Her stomach could have to wait; it could sound as angry as it wanted to, but she would not budge on her decision.

Gathering herself from the sudden scare, she looked away from the plate of food and back to the darkness of the hallway. She swiftly moved from the room and into the hall, clutching upon no more cobwebs or stepping on no more plates of mysteriously warm food.

Perhaps it was the swiftness of her motion, or perhaps it was something more, but the bedroom door creaked to a shut behind her, startling her.

Her feet carried her with swiftness down the dark, dusty, lonesome hallway. She took no more time to examine the scenery. Instead, she focused on the stairway ahead – something that would lead her downstairs to the front door.

Down the stairs, she fled with intensity. She could feel some of the steps wanting to give in beneath her weight, but she did not let that stop her. Before long, she was at the bottom, standing in the main foyer.

The exit was only a few yards away from her, and she hurried toward it. Natalie could feel her heart beating a mile a minute but she did not feel faint. She only felt the necessity of escaping this tragic castle. Gasping hold of the doorknob, she opened the door wide and placed one foot outside.

"Stop!" a voice beckoned from behind her, stopping her in her tracks. She froze, afraid to face the voice's source. "Please... don't go."

It was a man's voice – strong but not terribly threatening. Natalie released the door and stood still in her place.

"Please, do not go," the voice repeated. "It's... it's been so long since I've had any visitors."

At that moment, she knew that it was the infamous monster of the castle speaking to her.

A tinge of courage struck Natalie and she found the strength to turn around, albeit slowly. When she did, she could see the shadowed figure standing at the bottom step of the grand staircase. She could not see his face; only his form.

"You are the... master of this castle?" She chose her words carefully, almost using the term 'beast.'

"Aye," he announced with a low but trembling voice. "I have lived here alone for many a year."

"And it was you who brought me inside?"

"I – I could not leave you unconscious on my front steps. I brought you in. I put you to bed in one of the rooms."

Natalie was not sure how to reply. He seemed sincere, but she had heard so many horrible stories about the castle's monster that those rumors began plaguing her thoughts.

"Tell me, my lord, why you have remained in this castle alone for so many years?" she asked. Her curiosity was always much grander than her fears.

"Because," he began, "this is my home. It has been my home since the moment I was born onto this earth."

She nodded her head, wondering if he could see the motion. Even the bit of daylight from the open door did little to illuminate her presence.

"I apologize for intruding on your home, but my intrusion is over. I must return to my own home now."

Again, she turned to toward the door, but again she could hear his voice plea for her to stay.

"Just a moment longer, please," he begged. "For tea? For conversation? For nothing else but to amuse a man who has been left alone for so many years?"

"For amusement?" she chided, facing his shadowed image once again. "Is that how I am portrayed? As amusement?"

"No," he bumbled. "Never. You – you are…"

"I am what?" she demanded, stepping forward just a bit. "I am a humble but dignified lady, my lord. I am here neither for your pleasure nor your amusement."

"Then, might I ask, why are you here? Why is this your second visit to my castle in a mere week? No one else has the gall to visit such a place, much less twice."

"I am here for the same reason that I know you assume. I am here to see if the monster of the castle actually exists."

The lord of the castle said nothing at first, adding an uncomfortable silence through the thickness of the already uncomfortable confrontation.

Finally, he spoke. "Well, you have now met this 'monster.' Are you content? Are your myths and your rumors true?"

Uneasily, yet with a sense of determination, Natalie slowly began to approach him.

"I am unsure," she said, carefully choosing her words. "You seem nothing more to me but a mere man."

The lord also began to step closer. "A mere man? Hah! There is nothing mere about me, my lovely peasant."

"I've heard big men speak big words before. That does nothing to astonish me."

"Well, how is this for astonishment?"

With just the glimmer of light from the open door, he moved even closer, and for the first time, Natalie could see his burned, disfigured face.

With a start, she threw a hand to her chest and stumbled back. The man began to laugh as she scurried back to the door.

"That's right! Run! Run away like everyone else has!"

Out the door, Natalie flew, frightened and startled by what she had seen. She had only been able to see a small portion of his face, but it resonated within her, and as she ran, it was all that she could see. Horrified, she flew from the castle and down the massive hill that overlooked the village of Foliage.

Once she arrived back to the foot of town, she stopped and allowed herself to rest and breathe. What had she seen? Who had she seen? There were so many questions flooding her thoughts, but the shocking terror of the image in her head overwhelmed all else.

On unsteady legs, she walked to the fountain and rested atop its marble base. She tried hard to catch her breath – tried to hold back what seemed to be unreasonable tears – but she was unmistakably shaken.

"My, my, you look terribly shaken," said a voice from beside her. Turning her face, Natalie looked into the eyes of Madame Howell.

"Just – just a bit of over-exertion," Natalie announced. "I'll be fine, Madame."

Madame Howell stared at her and looked her over. "Why, you look as if you've seen a monster."

"I went for a walk that turned to a run, Madame," Natalie replied. "I'm just a bit winded."

"You know, child, the only monsters in the world are real people," the witch informed her. "Sometimes, they're the most beautiful people of all. And sometimes, the ones we think are monsters – well, they have the most beauty within."

Natalie stood there, quiet for the moment. She could hear Madame Howell's words, but she was uncertain of what she was referencing. It would have been impossible for the woman to have known Natalie had been at the castle, or that she had met its disfigured owner.

"I will let you be on your way," the old woman said. She gave Natalie a wink of the eye and a pat on the shoulder as she went about her business.

"Was the witch giving you trouble?" she heard a voice ask from across the fountain. When she looked, she saw a surprise that made her forget completely about the horrid castle on the hill.

"Willem Grillis," she whispered, catching his eye. "I am surprised to see you out with your ball only a day away."

"Then this is the best time to be out, isn't it?" he asked, flashing a bold but charming smile. "You still haven't answered my question, you know."

"Oh," she paused, as she had forgotten what his question was. His piercing eyes had distracted her.

"The witch?" he questioned, cocking one of those piercing eyes.

"Oh, yes, Madame Howell," she stammered. "No, Madame Howell is a kind old lady. She was just saying hello."

"I have heard she has a reputation for chaos," Willem countered. "I have heard some of the elder townspeople speak of her, and in her day, Madame Howell was a great healer. They say that as she aged, her mind started to go, and now all of her spells and potions go awry."

"Awry?" She wondered how awry a kindly old woman could get.

"Your parents drank wine and ended up asleep in a tree. Tell me, please, that magic had nothing to do with this."

"Yes," she answered. "Perhaps the wine was enchanted. It was wine and I have never had any. I do not know the effects, so I cannot really answer your question."

"I heard your father injured himself falling from the tree. Perhaps the enchanted wine was intended to do him in?"

"My father survived the fall just fine," she answered. "He is dead though. He died in a fire shortly after. His whole shop is gone. My mother is meeting with the Priest today." She said it all so fast that she wondered if she had actually said it or not. Willem stared back blankly.

"Oh, Natalie," he began, and it was apparent that he was having to search for his words. "I am terribly, terribly sorry. I had not heard this. Is there anything I can do – anything for you, or your poor mother?"

"No," she said. "We are both fine. Things will progress and change, but we will always be fine."

"I know what I can do for you!" he announced,

straightening and taking her hand. "I will save a dance at the ball just for you, Natalie. I will sweep you away on the dance floor and send your heart aflutter with my graceful waltzing and the whispering of sweet nothings into your ears!"

Pulling her to him, he began to swirl her around the cobblestone ground, humming music as he lead her in an impromptu waltz.

Looking into her eyes, he said, "People will adore you – they will adore us! We will be the image of magic in its truest form. All eyes will envy us. You will be the object of jealousy for every girl there."

While it all sounded very flattering and – though she hated to admit it – a bit romantic, Natalie's response was not as grand as she assumed Willem would have preferred.

"I will most gladly accept your offer for a dance," she began, "but I do not hope jealousy on anyone. I would hope they would be happy for me, to dance with the most handsome man at the ball. It is, after all, just one dance."

"Well…" he clamored as they stopped dancing. His eyes were like that of an excited child or a puppy dog needing attention. "A dance is more than just a dance, after all."

"How so?"

"A dance between two people is a connection. Yes, a

connection of their two spirits. It is a beautiful thing, really. Truly beautiful."

"And tell me, Sir Grillis, how many other spirits might you be connecting with during your ball?"

Her words had left Willem speechless. He continued to smile, but he was blushing also, which meant that Natalie had somehow embarrassed him. This made her smile as well.

"You know that I will be honored to dance with you tomorrow. And thank you," she said, gesturing a hand toward the ground, "for that marvelous taste of what our waltz will be like. You are a true gentleman."

Willem's eyes seemed to lighten at this and his smile grew to grand full perfection. Gracefully, he took Natalie's hand and bowed to kiss it.

"You humble me," he told her. "I will show you. You, my dear lady, will have the most wonderful time. I assure it."

"Okay," said Natalie, nodding her head. "I will take you up on it."

"Splendid! I must be off now, Natalie, but tomorrow – tomorrow we dance for all eyes to see!"

Giddy and almost animated, he bowed again and hurried off, disappearing quickly out of sight.

Natalie laughed. Although she would have rather not

admitted it, she had been flattered by Willem's gesture. Whereas he had offended her some with his allegations of Madame Howell, he had quickly redeemed himself through an impromptu waltz and a kiss to her hand.

"I doubt a young man could be more charming," she said, speaking only to herself as she sat on the stone ledge that wrapped around the fountain. "He's rather kind, and kindness goes a long way when looking to whom I could imagine spending my life with."

It was in this moment that Natalie reflected on her earlier thoughts of Willem Grillis and his family. She had worried of the possibility of them losing their family fortune, but she realized that Willem could survive the poorer life if he had to – especially if Natalie was there to show him how.

She felt somewhat sickened by the thought. Whereas most girls, she knew, would be fantasizing over how to spend the Grillis fortune and adjust to the life of the wealthy, Natalie was fantasizing about the Grillis' losing their wealth and being made to learn the ways of the poor.

"No one should wish a thing on anyone," she said.

"No one should wish what on anyone?"

The words came from Lord Jensen, as he approached her with his carriage driver walking a few paces behind him.

"Lord Jensen," Natalie said, standing and offering a curtsey. "My apologies. I did not know anyone was listening to my rambling."

"It does not matter," he said, looking the young girl over. Grunting, he tapped his cane against the stone ledge of the fountain. "Your father – he is dead?"

This question came as a surprise. Well, not the question itself so much, but the way Lord Jensen had delivered it – the bluntness.

"Yes," she whispered, looking to the ground. "His shop burned. He did not survive the fire."

"And his service? Will there be a funeral?"

"On Sunday, sir. My mother is with Father Harris now finalizing the arrangements."

"I'm going to visit them immediately then," the old man said. "Your family will have nothing to worry about. I will handle the financial end of laying your father to rest and repairing his shop. I trust you will be taking over the family business?"

"The candle shop?" she asked, speechless. "Lord Jensen, my mother and I could never ask –"

"And so you didn't," he said, interrupting her. "You will reopen your father's business and carry on his legacy in this town. I will supply everything that you need. I will not require a cent of payment in return."

"My lord," she pleaded, "my mother would never accept such an offer. She's a proud woman."

"She is a proud woman," he noted, nodding his head. "A lovely, proud woman."

His smile gave it all away. Natalie had never seen Lord Jensen smile, but now she understood. He was in love with her mother.

"I must be off," he said, nodding at her and tipping his hat. "Oh, before I go – does Roselyn enjoy a nice wine?"

Remembering the events that followed Madame Howell's gift of wine, she responded, "Not wine, perhaps, but she loves flowers."

"Flowers," he said in a grunt, nodding once more. "Flowers it is."

Natalie hid her smile behind her hand as she watched Lord Jensen and his driver depart. His conversation had given her something to think about – her family would need to make an income; having the shop up and running again would help with that. Natalie had interned under her father for years. She knew the ins and outs of the candle business.

But was that what she wanted to do for the rest of her life?

Leaving the fountain, she walked to the public market area

and noticed that most of the women with businesses there were unmarried – either spinsters or widows. Had they never found love? Could she not have both – a husband and a business?

"Husband," she whispered, thinking about her mother and how she would react to Lord Jensen's arrival with flowers and a fortune. Would her mother fall in love with him, and if she did, would they marry? Her mother would be in the same situation that Natalie had imagined herself in with Willem – a poor girl marrying into wealth. Her mother would be taken care of, and the candle shop would go to provide only for Natalie, and for Natalie alone.

"I'm going to be an old spinster," she said, gulping and looking down to the remains of the Wax Shoppe. "I do not mind honoring my father, nor do I mind running a business, but the thought of doing it alone – of going through life alone… is that really what I am here for?"

She spotted Sarah St. John by the florist's stand, chatting with Lord Jensen. This made Natalie cringe, as she hoped that she and her family's tragedy were not a part of their conversation. Once, the two quit speaking, Natalie caught Sarah's eye and the girl quickly walked to her.

"Natalie!" Sarah pleaded with a fresh, lively voice. "Natalie, please. This is the last chance! I will send my driver for you in the morning. You simply must let me have my stylist do your hair for the ball."

Feeling self-conscious from her spinster fantasy, she reconsidered Sarah's offer, even though accepting anything from Sarah was always against her better judgment.

"Is your stylist really as good as you say?" she asked.

"Like I told you, my father only employs the best. Meet me here in the market for tea and then we will get the hairstyles of our dreams!"

The offer sounded too good to be true, but Natalie no longer wished to look a gift horse in the mouth. She worried about being alone for the rest of her life, and if a professional hairstyle would help bring notice to her at the ball – there was nothing wrong with trying.

"I will be here," Natalie agreed.

"Wonderful. You will see!" Sarah turned to leave, yelling over her shoulder, "Tea! Don't forget."

Natalie wanted to doubt Sarah's intentions, but it was possible that the girl understood that Natalie was mourning the loss of her father, and it was possible that Sarah was sincere. Perhaps whatever conversation she'd had with Lord Jensen had awakened the kindness that was inside of her.

"Ha!" Natalie laughed. She had never known Sarah to be kind unless it benefitted her in some way. So, the real question was: how would Sarah helping with Natalie's hair benefit her?

For a brief moment, she considered standing Sarah up, but she decided to trust her. Perhaps if she trusted her this one time, they could actually be friends.

11

When she arrived home, there was no sign of Lord Jensen's carriage or of Father Harris's horse. Upon entry, there was also no sign of her mother. Natalie immediately noticed the bouquet of carnations near the fire place and it made her smile. Although she was still mourning her father – she knew that she would always mourn him. She wanted her mother to be happy, and if an old codger like Lord Jensen was the one that could make her happy, then she had no place to interfere.

"Mother?" she called questioningly. Moving through the humble, small homestead, she found no sign of Roselyn. "Mother, are you home?"

Perhaps, she thought, her mother had left with Lord Jensen. Perhaps they had gone out for a bite to eat and a spot of tea.

There were three empty tea cups on the table. Obviously, they had not gone out for more tea.

Walking to her bedroom, she sat on the edge of her bed and looked over to the mask that she would wear to the ball. It shimmered at her through all of its magical, enchanted glory.

"I wonder," she began, standing and moving to the mask, "will I meet my soulmate, or am I putting my faith in make-believe?"

Looking outside, she saw that she still had an hour or so before dark. That was plenty of time to visit the old witch, as Natalie had many questions for her, and not all of them revolved around the mask. Natalie was curious, as most young people were, about magic and powers and the craft. She did not think that she, herself, was a witch. She was also not afraid that Madame Howell was a witch. She was, however, very curious as to the extent of Madame Howell's powers. What all could the old woman do?

"I wonder," she thought aloud again, "if she could turn people into toads or snakes. Can she make the dead rise or fire fall from the sky?"

She knew as long as she was standing alone in her room, her curiosity would get her nowhere. Yet, she dared not move a step because she remembered that the last time she was curious about something, she ended up face to face with the castle's beast.

"He had seemed friendly enough," she admitted. "I wish I hadn't run away so fast. I – I was frightened. It was all so sudden and I had not expected to see him... to see his burns."

She wondered whom she was confessing to. There was no one there but her. There was no one to hear her apology of ignorance, and there was no one there to forgive her. It was not Madame Howell that she needed to visit; it was the beast in the castle.

"I must hurry," she said, wrapping a light cloak around her and taking her lantern. "I'll never make it there and back before nightfall."

She considered leaving her mother a note, but decided against it. The last thing that she wanted was to worry her mother further. A note saying that she had ventured to the feared castle would have likely sent her mother over the edge.

It was dusk when she made it to the crooked mountain with the dismal castle atop it. The village's marketplace had already closed for the day, and she had not seen a single person as she passed it – not even her mother.

Fog had emerged and filled the space around her with a texture that reminded her of the smoke that had killed her father. Still, she could breathe through this fog just fine – its comparison to smoke, however, gave her chills.

She decided against lighting her lantern now. There was just enough light for her to be able to see to reach the castle, and she worried that if anyone was lurking about, her lantern would have served only to draw attention to her. Natalie figured she'd had enough negative attention for one lifetime.

With careful strides and keeping herself wrapped in her cloak, Natalie began the climb up to the monster's castle, although it was her that felt like the monster now. The poor man, she thought, had only yearned for company, and after one look at him, she had fled. She was no better than the people who made fun of the castle's lord behind his back. She felt ashamed, and she hoped that he would forgive her.

As she approached the castle, she heard voices. These voices belong to young men – people around her own age. They did not belong to the lord.

"Who's there?" she asked, masking her fear as she approached. As it grew darker, she could only make out shadows.

"Well, what's this?" she heard one voice ask. Then, she could see three shadows begin to move toward her.

"It's that red-headed girl," a second voice answered.

"She's a freak," replied the third. "Look at her curly hair."

Then, once they stopped, she could see them. One of them was Luke St. John – Sarah's brother. The other two where his dimwitted thugs… his *henchmen*, she thought of them as.

"Oh, I know her," Luke acknowledged. "This is one of my sister's friends. She says she's trouble and messes with witches."

"I've heard all about you," one of the henchmen – Wilber, she remembered his name being – announced. "You've been to this castle before. Is the beast your boyfriend?"

"She's a witch," said the other henchman, Jonathan.

"Witches can't have boyfriends, you idiot."

"If you're a witch," Luke said, "show us. Show us your powers."

"I am not a witch," Natalie replied, feeling more nervous now.

"Liar!" Luke shouted, taunting her. "Show us. Everyone knows witches can fly. Show us you can fly. Fly off this mountain!"

"I – I can't fly," Natalie told them. She found herself having to back up as the three boys approached her.

"You can," Luke said. "All witches can fly. Everyone knows that."

"I'm not a witch!"

"If you won't show us on your own," Luke threatened, "then we will make you show us."

In about as long a time as it took her to blink, the boys charged her, pushing her closer and closer to the edge of the mountain.

"She's not going to show us," said Jonathan. "I say we just make her."

Natalie closed her eyes and swallowed. She could feel that her death was only moments away and that she would soon be reunited with her father. She thought of her mother and how distraught she would be.

No, Natalie did not want to die. She did not want to leave her mother. Instead, she wanted to cry and run away, but she was outnumbered and in a moment, she would likely be ripped to shreds or – at worst – stoned to death.

All because she had befriended Madame Howell.

Stillness surrounded her through the darkness of her closed eyes. Quiet. Not a sound. Not a peep. Not a motion or anything hitting against her body.

She was nervous and unsure of what to do. Slowly, she opened her eyes. It was fully dark outside now, and although the fog was below the mountain's ledge, she could see no one in front of her.

"Hello?" she asked, taking a daring step forward.

"You should run," a rough but distinct voice told her, and she recognized it immediately. It belonged to the lord of the castle.

"Are they gone?" she asked, looking for him but not seeing him.

"I said run!" he shouted, throwing a start into her.

Natalie did as she was commanded. She fled as fast as she could down the dark mountain, not once considering lighting her lantern. She did not stop for breath or slow her speed. Once, she skidded, but she caught herself and continued at as fast a pace as she could until she had reached the bottom.

Out of breath, she finally stopped. Her mind was racing, but it still had to catch up with the quick pounding of her heart. She pinched herself – yes, she was still alive. Natalie was in the dark over what had happened. One moment, three boys were about to send her falling to her death. The next moment, they were gone and the voice of the beast had replaced them.

Despite the treatment Luke and his friends had shown her, she hoped that they were alive. Then again, she was everlastingly thankful to the beast – no, the master of the castle – for saving her life. She had treated him badly, and yet he had saved her. She was indebted to him.

"I just wish I'd been able to apologize for my early treatment of him," she mumbled as she walked alone on her route home. "I will visit him again – first thing after Father's service on Sunday. I will thank him and I will keep him company. It is, after all, the least I can do."

There was a glow coming from the front window of her home and she knew that her mother was there. Stepping inside, she forced any fear or angst from her near-death adventure away from her and left it outdoors. Roselyn sat in the old chair near the fireplace, knitting a blanket.

"Everything is all set for Sunday," she said. "Father Harris really is a Godsend."

"I'm so glad," Natalie answered, kissing her mother on the cheek. "And Lord Jensen? Was he helpful at all?"

Roselyn smiled but did not take her eyes away from her knitting.

"Lord Jensen did say he saw you at the market today."

"He says that he wishes to restore the Wax Shoppe," she told her mother, knowing this would not be new information for her.

"Yes, he told me so."

"He also says that he intends for me to run it," Natalie added.

"Would that be so bad?" her mother queried. "You know how to do it – you've been in that shop ever since you were little."

"Yes, but Mother," she pleaded, "I don't want to be like those other women in the marketplace."

"What do you mean?"

"I don't want to die alone."

Roselyn looked up from her knitting this time. Natalie had tears welling in her eyes. She tried to force them back, but she could not.

"What are you talking about?"

Natalie cleared her throat and wiped a tear away. "They're

all alone, mother. All of the women who have businesses at the market – they're all alone. Every last one of them."

"But child, you don't have to be them. Having a business does not doom you to a life of loneliness."

Natalie nodded. Her mother always spoke with wisdom. "Will you be lonely, Mother?" she asked. "Without Father?"

Roselyn set her knitting aside and stood. She walked over to her daughter and placed her hands on the girl's shoulders. Looking into her eyes, she said, "How could I ever be lonely with such a wonderful daughter in my life?" Then, she hugged her close.

Natalie let the tears run free now. She did not mean to, but they came like a force and she collapsed into her mother's arms, sobbing like a scared little girl. This was because she was a scared little girl. Her father was dead. Her life had just been threatened, and she still felt terrible about running out on the beast – no, the lord of the castle.

"I think you and I just need to spend some quality time together, girl," Roselyn said, patting her on the hair and stroking her curly hair. "Tomorrow when I do your hair for the ball, we can chitchat like the old days and talk about handsome boys and mean girls."

"Oh, no," Natalie whispered with a start and pulled away

from her mother. "Oh, mother."

"Do you not want to talk about boys with me? Are you too old for that now? You're only eighteen, girl."

"No, it's not that," she said. "It's just – well…"

"Out with it."

"I agreed to let Sarah St. John's stylist do my hair tomorrow."

She braced herself, knowing she had probably just scarred her mother's feelings.

"Sarah St. John?" her mother said, repeating the name. There was a tinge of surprise in her voice, but Natalie could not see disappointment in her eyes. "I thought the two of you despised each other."

"So did I. I think Natalie feels bad over Father's death. She's been making efforts to be kind to me. I figured, since the effort was there…"

"I agree fully," her mother said, nodding her head in approval. "Perhaps you and Sarah have just misread one 'another over the years. I bet you could be the best of friends."

"I wouldn't push it that far," Natalie laughed. "But I do want to take her up on her offer. Her father has brought in a top stylist from Paris. Can you imagine, Mother? Paris – my hair will be done in the greatest fashion."

"I could not be more excited for you."

The two hugged again – this time without tears. Natalie felt better about her arrangement with Sarah, but she did not find the need to worry her mother with the events that had happened between herself and Sarah's brother and friends. That would have only worried – or angered – Roselyn, and Natalie was enjoying the warmth and peace of their current demeanor.

"Are you hungry?" her mother added. "There is bread and jam, eggs and some pork belly on the table for you. I cooked earlier, and I have eaten, but you must be famished."

Natalie hated to disappoint her mother, but she was not very hungry at all. As she declined the food and retreated to her room, her mind was occupied with tomorrow's ball, the hair appointment, and the concern that once Luke told Sarah what had happened at the castle, there would be no hair appointment nor would she be allowed entrance to the ball.

That was, if Luke had survived to tell his story.

The thought terrified her. Had blood been shed to save her life? She hadn't heard anything – not a scream or a cry or even a whimper. There had been only silence ringing loudly throughout her ears. Perhaps, she thought, they had screamed but she had been too trapped in her own thoughts of death to have noticed. There was also the fact that it had been dark when she opened her eyes and she saw no one – nothing. She had left in a hasty retreat following the lord's command that even if there had been three dead bodies lying around, she would not have noticed them. One thing was certain – whether the boys were dead or alive, Natalie now had two things to tell the lord of the castle – that she was sorry, and that she was thankful to him.

Dressing for bed, she stared into her mirror at her head full of wild, red locks and curls. Her hair had looked decent this morning when she left for the market. Now, from the stress and events of the day, it was a mess. She wondered what Sarah's stylist would do to it – was there any hope for it?

Her freckles – she noticed them too, speckled flaws against her pale white complexion. The most adored girls in the village – the ones that everyone fawned over – were flawless.

"Flaws or not," she whispered, turning from the mirror, "they are mine and I love them."

She remembered that her father had called her freckles her little pops of sunrays. He had said they reminded him of the sun, and that they were part of what made her beautiful.

Natalie missed her father, and she knew she would always miss him.

Curling beneath her cover, she blew out the candle beside her bed and rested her head. She could hear the breeze outside as the shutters rapped against the house. Storms had often frightened her, but not on this night. It could have rained; the wind could have caused havoc. It would not have scared her. No, Natalie had been scared enough. She was tired of being afraid, and as she drifted off to sleep, her mind gave her peace and her dreams were all deservingly pleasant.

12

Even as her dreams were kind, Natalie awoke with a start. The heavy door of her bedroom burst open and her mother stampeded in, full of energy.

"Rise 'n shine, Natalie!" Roselyn called, opening the shutters and letting the fresh air and sunlight fill the room. Your breakfast is on the table." She gave her daughter a quick kiss on the forehead and added, "I have to be off now. Don't forget it's your turn to feed the hens."

"Where are you off to in such a hurry?" Natalie asked, rubbing the sleep from her eyes.

"Lord Jensen has offered to take me to the marketplace in a neighboring village. I want to pick up some food supplies for after your father's service tomorrow."

"That is very kind of Lord Jensen," Natalie said. "Will you be late?"

"Don't you worry, my sweet daughter," Roselyn replied. "I will be home in plenty of time to help you dress for the ball."

This gave Natalie comfort and she smiled as her mother left the room. She could smell the delicious scent of her breakfast from where she lay, and she sat up with a stretch and a yawn. Standing, she gazed in her mirror, looked at her hair – which was a ratty mess from sleeping on it – and hurried away to the table.

After eating, she bathed and dressed in a blue dress that her mother had made for her two years ago. It still fit fairly well, but she had grown a bit taller and so the dress seemed shorter. While she was modest about her ankles showing, she let it pass. Truth be told, Natalie did not know what to wear. She was meeting Sarah for tea, and they would hurry off to wherever her stylist had set up shop. Natalie did not see the point in getting dressed up twice in one day – she would look plain for Sarah, and then she would stun her at the ball.

"Mother is the greatest," she said, as she stepped out into the sunshine. "The dress she made is magnificent. If Sarah's stylist does his job, I may have a chance at wooing Willem after all."

Her confidence had received a boost. She had no other choice than to think as she was. She was not going to be alone for the rest of her life. She did not know if she loved Willem or not – actually, that was not true. She knew that she did not love him, as she barely knew him. Yet, she thought, perhaps, she could grow to love him. He was charming. He was handsome. He tried much too hard to be romantic, but it worked because it added to his charm. She still did not care too much for his fortune. It would have been a perk, of course, but she would be able to make her own income at the candle shop. She would not need his fortune to survive.

That thought came as a sudden relief to Natalie. It was the first time that she had taken in what Lord Jensen had truly offered – financial security. He had been so abrupt about it all that she had not fully grasped his intentions, but Lord Jensen had been a friend of her father's for many years, and he simply wanted to make sure that she was taken care of.

Perhaps, she wondered, that was his intention with her mother as well. Was he not being romantic with her? Of course not, she thought, kicking a pebble down the path. Now that she considered it all, he was simply making sure that Roselyn was taken care of also. It was all a very kind gesture from a man often considered cold and bitterly frank.

As she neared the center of the village, she could see Sarah St. John's horse drawn buggy parked along the walk. The driver waited inside it, but Sarah was not with him. Natalie glanced across the way, searching among the heads of the Saturday shoppers for a glimpse of her slightly less annoying nemesis.

She spotted her, already seated at a patio table outside the café. Although Natalie's brain was ready to trust Sarah, her body was not, and it walked toward Sarah with slow, cautious strides.

"Natalie!" Sarah exclaimed when she saw her. Standing, she greeted her guest. "I am so glad you could make it. I was terribly afraid that you would back out."

"Why would I back out?" she asked, sitting at the chair across of Sarah.

"Oh, now, do not take it personally," Sarah continued. "It's just – well – we all know how timid you are."

"Timid?" she questioned.

"You know, afraid to try new things."

New things… Natalie thought of how she had just recently visited the *beast's* castle, had her father die, nearly been pushed off a mountainside, and there was so much more still spinning and weaving around her. So far, she had held her own, but if the circle of change around her continued to escalate, she feared that she would not be able to keep up.

"Go on," she said, taking a sip from the tea that had been ready for her.

"Anyway, you're here now. So, after tea, we'll ride down to my father's studio where he has the stylist set up and ready for us."

"Your father's studio?"

"Yes," Sarah acknowledged. "You did not think that we would allow him to do it in our home, did you? There would be red hairs everywhere. It would take the servants days to find them all and clean them up."

There they were, Natalie thought – the insults. She had been waiting on them. She had known that it was only a matter of time.

"Of course," she commented, covering the sneer with a smile. "I would rather hate to shed or molt all over your home."

"I'm glad we agree then," Sarah added, smiling and sipping her tea. "We had better get going soon though. Who knows how long it will take to transform that hair of yours into something …presentable."

"Yes," Natalie chided, "who knows, indeed."

The rest of the tea time was brief, as Sarah was more rushed than usual. Natalie did not mind this. The last thing she wanted was to hear another insult.

Still, the insults came as they rode from the marketplace, but not once had Sarah mentioned her brother or his two friends. That likely meant that they were safe and sound, but if that were the case, why had they not spoken out about what had happened on the mountain?

Perhaps, she thought, they were too afraid. Perhaps the beast – no, the lord had frightened them so terribly that they were fearful of ever muttering a word about it. This thought made her grin, as those three boys had deserved worse than just a tongue lashing from their parents.

That was a joke; she knew that their parents .never would have punished them over what they could have done. Luke and his friends would never have spoken to their parents about Natalie's *fall* from the mountain. They never would have claimed to have been at the castle in the first place. Their deadly action would have gone forever unknown, had the lord of the castle not defended her.

She still ached to know exactly how he had stopped them.

"We're here," Sarah said, stirring Natalie from her thoughts.

Looking ahead, Natalie saw a glorious building made of stone and slate. It was large enough to have housed her home three times with room left over for a shed.

"My father employs many artists and sculptors, you know," Sarah pointed out. "Our private dressmaker works out of here as well. I was only taunting you about your hair earlier. This is where the stylist would be no matter who was coming."

Natalie was somehow moved by this, as it seemed Sarah had almost apologized for her rude comment over tea.

"Your father is a collector of art?" she asked her.

"The arts," Sarah corrected her. "Father is a great collector of the arts. He prides himself on his collection."

"Your father sounds like a very worldly man."

"Why, Natalie, I believe him to be one of the most worldly

men that there is."

Natalie could not blame her for having such esteem for her father; she had also felt the same about hers. In fact, she still felt the same.

The buggy pulled up to the entrance of the building, which was substantially large. Four pillars lined the entrance, and four marble steps led up to it.

"If my father's studio impresses you this much, I hate to see how you're going to react at the ball," Sarah said, laughing. "I know that it seems rather enormous, but that has a purpose. Sometimes rather large sculptures are created here, and they have to be placed on dollies and wheeled out. A ramp is fitted over the steps in those instances."

"That makes sense," Natalie whispered, but she had trouble imagining any sculpture being large enough to need such a gigantic passageway.

Then again, she had not traveled outside of the village much either.

Once inside, although still stunning, Natalie found it less impressive. There was a large open area in the center of the building, and there were two smaller rooms off to either side. It was definitely a building made of work stations. One of the doors had the sign "Seamstress" on it – the permanent studio of Sarah's dressmaker.

"We're this way," Sarah said, leading Natalie in the direction opposite of the dressmaker's studio. "Pierre will be delighted to see us. My father says he intends to create masterpieces on our heads."

"That sounds – interesting," Natalie replied. She was now more uncertain than ever that this was the right place for her to be.

Opening the door to the left, Sarah entered the room, holding the door while Natalie followed in behind her.

"Mademoiselle!" the flamboyantly attired French hairstylist said as they entered the room. "You be like ze most beautiful flower!"

"Thank you, Pierre," Sarah replied.

"And your friend – she has ze most beautiful red hair! C'est magnifique!"

Natalie blushed and half-way curtsied to the stylist. He smiled back with ecstatic emotion.

"Sarah, you must be first," Pierre continued. "I must take my time with ze red hair!"

"He's going to style me first," Sarah mumbled, shifting her eyes to the ground. Then, forcing a smile, she added, "You know how it is with these stylists. They like to get the easiest jobs out of the way first."

Natalie smiled along with her, but not because Sarah's hair would be easier, but because she could tell by her expression and tone of voice that how she had put it was not exactly how Pierre had put it.

As Pierre sat Sarah down in his chair, Natalie studied the room. She saw a mess of supplies spread across a table, and there were even more in an open bag on the floor beside the work station. There was a section dedicated to ribbons and flowers and the like, and a few other bags were scattered about but they were closed and Natalie could only guess to what they contained.

There was one thing that disturbed her. For all she could see, she could not find one mirror.

Making note of this, she said, "I do not see a mirror. How will we see what he does?"

"Pierre does not believe in mirrors," Sarah answered.

Pierre looked at Natalie and smiled. "Mirrors – ze are evil and ze steal your soul."

"Oh," whispered Natalie. She knew that it was not true, of course. She had stared into the mirror in her bedroom many a time, and she was pretty certain that her soul was still intact and present.

Sitting down in a chair near the supply bags, she watched Pierre work his French magic on Sarah's golden locks. When he had finished, her golden locks were even more spectacular than ever. They wove around two braids that started at her widow's peak and draped her forehead to either side. He tied it off with a lavender ribbon, which Natalie assumed he had been told would match Sarah's dress.

"How do I look?" Sarah asked her, smiling giddily. "Is it beautiful, Natalie? Oh, please tell me! Please tell me if it's beautiful."

Not having to fib even a little, Natalie was pleased to say, "You look stunning, Sarah. He truly did create a masterpiece."

Natalie, herself, was relieved at this, as it helped wipe away concerns of Pierre doing anything drastic or frightful to her hair.

"Oh, Natalie," Sarah continued, "I hope Willem will like it. Do you think he will like it?"

Natalie hated the question, but she hated more the honesty she was portraying. "He will love it," she said, feeling that it was truthful even though it saddened her.

As Sarah moved from the chair by Pierre, Pierre ushered for Natalie to approach.

"Mademoiselle, you are to become a work o' art," he said. "You shall be ze most stunning of my creations."

Natalie knew that her time had come. Graciously, she approached the chair and sat. Then, closing her eyes, she let Pierre work his magic. The process seemed to take a bit longer than it had with Sarah, but Natalie had expected this. She had more hair of the two, which gave Pierre more to work with. She only hoped that when he was finished, her style was half as outstanding as Sarah's new look.

When Pierre was finished and Natalie stood from the chair, she looked to Sarah with questioning eyes.

"I've never seen you look so beautiful," Sarah said, admiring the style.

"Really?" Natalie asked, feeling relieved and thankful. Softly, she reached a hand to her hair.

"Non!" Pierre shouted, throwing a hand to his heart. "You must not touch. It must set."

Natalie obliged, as she was thankful for his work and did not want to risk destroying it. She would be able to see it for herself when she returned home, which she was most excited about. What kind of masterpiece had Pierre created for her? She did not dare ask Sarah, as she wanted to be surprised – to be floored – when she marveled at it in her mirror for the first time.

After bidding thanks and farewell to Pierre, Natalie and Sarah boarded the buggy and began the venture into the village. Natalie was beginning to feel a change in her opinion of Sarah. Perhaps she had misjudged her all along. It was true that Sarah was privileged and a bit spoiled because of it, but she had just given

Natalie a truly wonderful gift to help lighten her from the crisis her family was currently suffering. Only someone with a good heart deep inside would have done that, she knew, and she believed that Sarah was perhaps a decent person on the underneath.

"You know," Sarah said, breaking a silence that had formed since they left the studio, "I had a thought."

This sent a shiver down Natalie's skin.

"Do you remember my brother Luke?"

Natalie felt her heart stop. Her ears clogged and all sound turned into a low buzzing. Sarah's mention of her brother's name alone had nearly killed her.

"Yes," she whispered, swallowing her fear.

"I know he is only sixteen, but he will be at the ball tonight also with some of his little friends. I imagine you will be arriving without an escort and I am certain he would be willing to dance with you, if you'd like."

Natalie felt both relief and further fear. She had not expected Luke to attend the ball, and she was more thankful now than ever that she would be wearing a mask.

"Whereas I do appreciate the offer," she replied, choosing her words as wisely as she could, "I must decline."

"Why?" Sarah questioned, and her eyes darted into Natalie's like spears into fish. "Do you not find him handsome enough?"

"It's not that at all," Natalie said. Now was a good time for her to fib, she suspected. "My father recently passed away, and I am still in mourning. It – it would be disrespectful of me." Actually, as she said the words, she realized they were more honest than she had intended.

"Ah," Sarah said, nodding her head. "That is very honorable. Of course, I understand. It is a shame though."

"I agree," Natalie noted. "I'm sure Luke is quite the dancer."

"Forget about Luke," Sarah barked. "You won't be able to dance with Willem."

The words numbed her. Natalie felt the bite, and Sarah was the spider. She had found her tender spot – a spot in her scheme to avoid Luke... a spot that she had not otherwise considered.

"I imagine I will survive," Natalie whispered, feeling doomed by her own words. She knew that Sarah's eyes would follow her the entire night, and she would surely notice if she were to dance with Willem.

The driver brought the carriage to a stop at the foot of Natalie's drive. The carriage was much too large to fit down it.

"Thank you again," Natalie said, stepping from the buggy. "I cannot express my gratitude enough."

"Oh, the happy look on your face is thanks enough," Sarah replied.

Natalie waved goodbye as they disappeared into the distance.

The lights from within the house let her know that her mother was home from her excursion. Eager to show off her new hairstyle, Natalie raced up the horse-paved drive and to her home. She stepped inside quickly and shut the door behind her.

"You forgot to feed the hens," her mother said from the kitchen.

"I'm sorry, Mother," Natalie responded. "I was just so anxious – I forgot."

"No mind. I checked on them and fed them when I returned. Hungry little birds, they were."

"Thank you, Mother. I promise not to let it happen again."

"It's the big day," Roselyn said in her usual blunt and friendly tone. "You're allowed to be forgetful today. How did your hair turn out, by the way?"

"I don't know," she answered, crossing toward the kitchen. "I haven't seen it yet."

"Well, come 'ere and let me have a look at you."

As Natalie stepped into the kitchen, Roselyn's jaw dropped. Natalie stood still with a smile on her face, watching as her mother's eyes gazed upon her.

"It's that stunning?" she asked with great excitement. "Oh, Mother – I simply must go look!"

Hurriedly, she left her mother standing speechless in the kitchen while she ran into her bedroom. She pushed open her door and flung herself through the room and to her mirror. Anxious and giddy, she could feel her heart race with excitement and anticipation. When she looked into the mirror, her jaw dropped as well.

Her screeching, shrilling scream echoed throughout the small homestead.

Gazing at her reflection, she saw her hair, twisted here and puffy there, extended through frizzy strands straightened by small tree branches. There was a real bird's nest in one of the giant, alarming red mounds of puff. Dead butterflies were attached in other areas. There were dried flowers on her hair and buried within her hair, and weeds and leaves seemed to sprout from everywhere. It was not a beautiful sight. It was terrifying.

"Mother!" she shouted through her tears, falling to her knees in front of the mirror. "Mother! It's ruined. My hair is ruined!"

Roselyn rushed into the room and crouched down beside her daughter, placing a hand on her back. "It will be okay,

Natalie," she said, offering assurance. "We will comb this out. I know we can fix this."

"That rotten girl," Natalie said through her tears. "She let him do this to me. She had this planned all along! She's horrible mother – just horrible."

"Yes, she is," Roselyn said softly, holding her daughter close to her. "Sometimes the biggest monsters are the prettiest people."

Natalie stopped crying and opened her eyes. Pulling from her mother, she looked at her and asked, "What did you say?"

"I said that sometimes the biggest monsters…"

"Are the prettiest people…" Natalie stood, now understanding what Madame Howell had meant by the fountain. It was true. Sarah was the biggest monster Natalie had ever seen.

"First," Roselyn said, taking her hand, "let's get you dressed. Once you're dressed, we'll have time to work out this hair.

"What could they have been thinking, Mother?" Natalie asked. Frustration had reddened her complexion. "How could Pierre have thought *this* would look appropriate?"

"I – I don't know for sure," she said. "You and I – we come from a different world than Sarah St. John and her French friend. Maybe where Pierre is from, what he did to you would be loved and admired."

"But not at this ball, Mother. I'll be the laughing stock and Sarah knows it."

It took some effort, but Roselyn calmed Natalie down enough to help her dress. Before touching the hair, she added a touch of light pink to Natalie's lips and tied a strand of cream-colored pearls around her neck to match the dress.

"Mother," she gasped, touching upon the necklace, "this is the strand that father gave you."

"He gave those pearls to me when you were born," Roselyn said with pride in her voice. "I want you to have them now, and I know he would want the same."

Natalie was touched. It meant even more to her than the dress that she currently wore. Gazing into the mirror, she saw how the pearls on the necklace and the ones on the dress were the perfect match.

"Now, let's get this mess of hairstyle under control," Roselyn added. "And then, you go to that ball and steal that boy right out from under that witch of a friend of yours."

Natalie could not tell her mother why she wouldn't be dancing with Willem at his ball, but she did not concern herself with that at the moment. Instead, she settled in a chair while her mother attempted to repair her hair.

She could feel Roselyn pulling at her, twisting things and working a brush. After a moment, she heard her grunt.

"What's the matter?" Natalie asked.

"Your hair is stiff as a board," she answered.

Natalie remembered Pierre's orders to let the hair settle. She wondered what he had put in it.

Roselyn stood and left the room. When she returned, she held a pair of scissors.

"What are you doing with those?" Natalie asked, eyeing the scissors suspiciously.

"Well, it's either this or you're the bird lady for a while," Roselyn answered, snipping the scissors in the air for emphasis. "I'm fine with either one. I won't be the one walking around with branches and a nest on my head."

There was nothing Natalie could do. In all her life, she had never had a good haircut. Her untamed frizzy curls had always fought any style attempted. She was fearful of what she would look like once her mother was done, but she knew that it had to be better than how she currently looked.

Being bald would be better, she thought.

Although her mother – unlike Pierre – gave her the option of watching through the mirror, Natalie could not bear it. She trusted her mother – a great deal more than she trusted anyone else in this world. She did not need to watch in order to know that her mother would not deceive her as Sarah and her stylist had.

There were several snip snips and many clip, clip, clips, and there was more tugging and pulling and ripping than Natalie wanted.

"I should go get the handsaw from the shed," Roselyn said, jokingly.

Natalie did not see the joke in it, and eyes grew wide with fear.

More snips and clips and pulls and tugs... rips and shreds and the breaking of branches – a dead butterfly fell to Natalie's feet, halfway torn in two. Dead flowers joined it, as did a bird's nest and a stuffed bird that neither she nor her mother had noticed earlier.

"How could you not know he was doing this?" her mother insisted as she tried to make gold from sawdust.

"He had no mirrors," she explained with a pout.

"Never trust someone who does not believe in mirrors," Roselyn added. "That means they do not trust themselves enough to see themselves the way everyone else sees them."

Natalie did not reply, but she heard the truth in her mother's words.

Soon, her mother wet her hair and then dried it with a

towel. Natalie could then feel the brush run more freely through her hair, although it got caught up in a knot here and there. Those knots were stripped away, and once her entire head of hair – or what remained of it – had been brushed loose, round four began.

There was more snipping of the scissors, which continued to worry Natalie. There was more pulling and separating, but not tearing or shredding anymore. There was twisting, and there was stretching. Then she felt tying, which radiated her curiosity further.

After Roselyn patted her on the head, Natalie looked at her as she stepped in front of her. Roselyn stared down at her with a grand smile and bright eyes.

"You look radiant," she said. "Please, look in the mirror."

Natalie was still afraid of what she would see, but she did as her mother told her, and she turned to the mirror. There, her eyes gazed at her reflection, and just as before, her jaw dropped. This time, however, it did not drop from shock or horror or disgust. No, this time it dropped from awe – an awe that was of the sheer beauty her mother had created.

No longer were there signs of anything Pierre had done; there was no frizz, no awkward, messy curls, and no giant masses of hair flowing around her back and shoulders. Her hair had been tamed – controlled and brought to a new life. There were still curls and locks, but there were also beautiful braids that wrapped her head like radiant strips of sunset. There were two locks of hair that fell at her temples, bouncing with perfect curl. At the top of her head, much of her hair was in a bun, wrapped and controlled with additional braids.

She had never looked more mature – more ravishing than in this very moment. Through the mirror, she could see her mother behind her now, staring also at her reflection in the mirror. Roselyn was smiling, and a few tears were trailing down her cheeks.

Roselyn took the mask that Madame Howell had made, and she placed it upon Natalie's face, securing it in the back with pins.

"You are certain to be the belle of the ball," Roselyn said.

"It's not too late for me to stay here with you tonight," Natalie plainly told her. "Tomorrow is when we lay Father to rest. I know how hard this must be for you."

"Whereas I appreciate the sentiment," her mother answered, "your father would be so angry with me if I were to let you do that. He knew how much this night means to you, and you will not miss it."

Natalie felt humbled and nodded. Then she noticed her mother's eyes turn curious.

"Oh, Natalie," she said in a distressed tone. "I feel so horrible."

"What is it mother?"

"With everything going on, I forgot to arrange a driver for you. Your father was going to do that."

"Nonsense, Mother," Natalie said. "It will be Wilma and me all the way."

"Wilma?" she asked.

"Yes."

"Your father's horse?"

"Yes."

"The one that has bucked you off of her every time you've tried to ride her? That Wilma?"

"The very one."

"Oh, my child," Roselyn pleaded, "you know that horse is a death wish. I am planning on selling her at the market next weekend."

"Wilma and I just need to come to an understanding," Natalie defended. "If I can prove to you that I can ride her tonight, may I keep her?"

It was her father's horse, after all. She did not want to give Wilma up without a fight – no matter how brutal the horse had been with her in the past.

"Throw a blanket over her, at least," Roselyn relented. "If she bucks you off one time though, she's gone next Saturday."

"Deal," Natalie replied. She swallowed at the thought,

hoping that she knew what she was doing.

13

Roselyn led Natalie to the small stable in the barn. The sound of chickens clucking filled the air. The barn was dim inside, and Roselyn lit a lantern near the stall. The glow from the lantern shone into the stall and onto Wilma. The horse was, in fact, a Dales Pony, and she was rather large for her breed – tall, wide and heavy.

"Hello, Wilma," Natalie said, approaching the stall.

Wilma grunted at her and shook her head.

"Wilma, I need you to trust me tonight. You see, Father is not here, and I need your help."

Wilma was silent. Her black eyes glistened from the glow of the lantern.

"I need you to let me ride you tonight," Natalie continued. "I know that I am not your favorite person, but for once in your life, I need you to trust me."

Natalie looked at the quiet horse and wondered if Wilma had understood anything she was saying. Then, Wilma grunted again, huffed loudly, and pawed one hoof over the ground. Natalie caught Wilma's stare – it was one that warned her to not make one wrong move.

Roselyn stepped aside as Natalie opened her stall gate.

Then, she too moved aside as Wilma walked toward them. As Wilma walked through the opening and passed Natalie, she shot her another stare.

Natalie watched as the horse walked ahead of her, stopping by the stump that her father used to stand on and climb on top of her.

"Well, she's well trained," Natalie noted, walking toward Wilma.

"Please, be safe," Roselyn said.

"Mother, it is just a simple ball," Natalie said in a comforting tone. "You have absolutely nothing at all to be worried of."

Turning from her mother, she threw a white blanket over Wilma's back and, from atop the stump, Natalie climbed on.

Wilma began to huff and grunt, but she was not bucking – yet.

"There, there, girl," Natalie whispered to her. Leaning forward, she settled onto her and clutched a bundle of hair on Wilma's neck. Looking back to her mother, she asked, "Are you sure you'll be okay here alone?"

"Yes," Roselyn answered. You – you be okay too, you hear me?"

Natalie smiled and nodded her head. Then, holding on

tight, she gave Wilma a command, and the horse began to trot. As Wilma gained speed, Natalie felt proud of herself – and she felt proud of Wilma too. The Dales had not tried to buck her even once. It was as if they'd met at a kindred level.

Or not. Once Wilma had found a speed that she liked, it seemed nearly impossible for Natalie to slow her down when they had to make turns. Three times, Natalie was almost thrown from the Dales from this – but not once from bucking.

Natalie wondered just how instinctive Wilma's senses were, because as they neared the Grillis Manor, the Dales slowed immediately down to a steady, soft trot. At the open gate, she stopped completely.

"Come on," Natalie said in an attempt to get Wilma to cross through the entrance. "There's nothing there. The gate is open."

Wilma grunted and backed away.

"Fine, I'll lead this time." Climbing down from Wilma, Natalie walked through the open-gate entrance. Once through the threshold, she turned back to the Dales. "You can either follow me through, wait there like a chicken, or run back home – but I would prefer you did not do that last thing. If so, Mother will sell you at the marketplace and I cannot assure that you won't be turned into food."

Wilma was quiet for a moment. Then, with a deep, breathy huff, she stepped off to a spot in the lawn near a tree began to graze.

"You lazy beast," she said, shaking her head. "Fine. Enjoy your meal. I am sure that I won't be too long."

She turned from Wilma and faced the long, winding drive that sloped up a hill. Although her shoes were not made for comfort, they still managed to serve her well, as she did not slip or stumble even once. Yet, halfway up, she came to a stop. It was the first time she had seen the Grillis Manor with her own two eyes, and it was quite the sight to behold.

Pillar after pillar stood at the grand entrance of this wide spanning, three story manor. The pillars, along with the steps, were white marble, and the building itself was maroon and gold. It was the most fantastic place she had ever seen, putting the awe that she felt over the St. John studio to shame.

She wondered how many servants it took to clean the windows.

Holding up the front of her dress enough so that the hem did not touch the ground, she walked again, continuing her journey toward those brilliant marble steps and the excitement that awaited her beyond them.

Along the top of the drive, many buggies and carriages sat

near empty – only their drivers remained to mind their horses. Natalie rolled her eyes at this, as her horse was napping at the bottom of the hill.

There were two doormen at the entrance. Neither of them spoke to her as she neared them, but in unison, they opened the double front doors for her so that she could enter. Once inside, she stopped. She heard the doors close behind her, and she knew that this was it – this was the moment she had been both craving and dreading.

The entrance hallway was as golden as the outside. A maroon carpet divided the room as it crossed down the middle of the floor from one door to the other. There were some of the grandest paintings she'd ever seen lining the walls – brilliant landscapes and impressive buildings. At the door on the far end, another doorman waited.

Natalie was frozen, nervous from the tip of her nose to the tip of her toes. She wanted to walk – really, she did. It just seemed impossible. The more that she looked to the end of the hallway and at the expressionless doorman, the distance grew longer and narrower to her. She felt dizzy, and her stomach gave her a warning sound. If she did not gain control of herself, she would surely get sick. This was neither the time nor the place for her to be ill.

She took a breath – a deep, long one – and closed her eyes with it. When she exhaled, it was nice and slow, and she opened her eyes with a fresh new breath.

With one small, unsteady step after another, she walked. She swallowed down her nervousness; she swallowed down her fear. She had, after all, come this far, and it would be tragic if she turned back now. Natalie was not a quitter. Neither of her parents had been quitters and they had not raised one.

She squared her shoulders as she walked. When she approached the doorman, she offered a curtsy. He bowed in return.

"Normally, I would announce you," he said politely, "but it is a masquerade ball and that would take away part of the mystery. Don't you think?"

Natalie was charmed at his enthusiasm, seeing as he – and the other staff – was not masked for the occasion.

The doorman then continued his job by opening the door for Natalie's entrance.

Stepping through the threshold, she fell into an immediate state of wonder. It was the grandest spectacle she had ever seen. She had apparently arrived a bit late, as the doorway opened into a beautiful, ornate ballroom, and it was full of the most intriguing guests with the most fantastic dresses and masks and tailored suits she could imagine.

With a bit of insecurity, Natalie took the slowest steps and came to a fearful halt as she heard the door close behind her.

She was thankful that there had been no guest announcements, as no one had yet seemed to notice her. Everyone was otherwise occupied, taking and chatting with friends and influential acquaintances.

Every eligible girl in the kingdom must have been here. Natalie's eyes gazed around at the most beautiful young women – laughing and talking with one another as they awaited their turn for a dance with Willem.

It was fine that she could no longer dance tonight, Natalie thought, as she moved to a shadowed corner of the room. She felt as if she had no chance with all of the richly tailored dresses and highly skilled mask creations. She felt they overshadowed her, and perhaps she was right.

Perhaps her dress had not been made by a top seamstress, and perhaps her mask was made by the hands of a witch instead of a skilled designer. None of that really mattered, she knew, because a top stylist had done her hair, and it had been the most terrible hairstyle she had ever seen. And then someone with no experience – her mother – had managed to transform the mess into something magnificent. That same woman was the woman who created her beautiful dress – a dress that she cherished much more deeply than any of the other girls possibly cherished theirs.

As for her mask – well, she much preferred a mask made by a witch than one made by the most talented designer on the globe. While the other masks around her may have had the greatest style, hers had a splash of witch's luck.

How odd for her to feel so at ease when she knew that the other girls in attendance were looking at her and, not even knowing who she was, judging her by her clothing. She could see them as they looked at her – their eyes darting from her dress to her mask to her hair; the way they sneered as they stared, whispering cruelties to one another.

She took it, letting her lips portray a smile from beneath the ridge of the mask. Natalie had no fear. She could leave whenever she wanted, and it would not be because of mean girls with nothing better to do than whisper about her.

A gentleman a few inches taller than her also found the shadowy corner and rested against the wall, just a few feet down from her. His suit was glistening of silver that had been woven with blue and black threads. His mask was encrusted in cut diamonds and blue satin. The jet black of his hair complimented it nicely.

"So," he asked – something she had not expected him to do. "Why are you not dancing? Are there no suitable men for your tastes?"

She was nervous to speak to him, but she did not show it. "I am certain there are plenty of suitable young men present. The ones I worry about are the ones in the shadows."

"And why is that?"

"I have to wonder why all the other girls have rejected him, of course."

With the slightest curtsy, she stepped away from the wall and left the curious gentleman in his shadow.

Would this be how she had to remain all night, she wondered – dodging every young man that requested a dance with her?

No, she thought, as she stopped in her place and looked around at every head she could. She recognized no one, and with the mask covering much of her face, no one would recognize her either. Even Sarah would not be able to spot her, she knew, as the last time Sarah had seen her, Natalie's hair had been a habitat for dead animals. This newfound knowledge pleased her as it meant that she would not have to bow out of every dance offered, and that she could even keep her dance with Sir Willem, if she could find him.

She walked around again, brushing elbows with masked person after masked person, engaging in no conversation as none was offered. Even though she could now dance freely, she was still somewhat insecure, as she realized that most of her friends were older than she and known through her parents and from the marketplace. Aside from Sarah St. John and her crew, it would not have mattered if everyone wore masks or not – Natalie would have known nearly nobody.

She felt the loneliness topple her insecurity. She was the wallflower of the ball. Those that were not chatting or dancing with their escorts were engaging in conversation with their friends.

Natalie imagined many of them were making new acquaintances at this ball, but she was not one for mingling with strangers. Truth be told, Natalie was an introvert, and there were few people that she desired to share the happenings of her life with.

She stopped as she caught the gaze of a young man in a suit and mask made in gold and white. His smile was marvelous, and without an invitation, he approached her. Natalie wanted to turn away, but she could not. His ecstatic emotion made her heart flutter.

"Miss Natalie," he said as he approached her. He took her hand and bowed to kiss it – something very familiar to Natalie. "I have been looking for you all evening."

She recognized him now – it was Willem Grilles.

"How did you know it was me?" she asked him as he stood and straightened.

"How could I not recognize your magical green eyes? I would know them anywhere. No mask could hide them from me."

Now, she was truly flattered. He had known her by her eyes, and that notion made her swoon.

"Oh, Willem," she said, "I am honored for your memory and for your keen vision."

"My lady," he added, "any man that forgets you is a fool."

Forget everyone else, Natalie thought, as they were all disappearing from her mind. All she could see was Willem, staring at her with his radiant eyes and profound smile. Perhaps, she wondered, would she truly have to *make* herself love such a man? For the first time, she could see how impressive he actually was and it made her crave a moment longer of his time.

As the music ended and the couples toward the center of the room parted from their dance, Willem took Natalie's hand.

"I believe I owe you a dance," he said, leading her as he moved through his other guests, toward the very center of the room. "This next dance – no matter what music is played – is sure to be the best dance."

"Why is that?" she asked, feeling nervous, as every eye was suddenly on her and Willem Grilles.

"Because it will be with you," his charming, soothing tone whispered. Then, his voice grew loud as he shouted behind him. "A waltz, however, would be splendid!"

And so, the music began again. Willem knelt before Natalie, holding her hand in his as he bowed his head. Then, kissing her hand, he stood with grace and dignity, embracing her in a formal waltz position.

Natalie had never imagined that she could move so gracefully – she had never danced a step in her life. She was allowing him to freely move her, and she listened as he counted to her, "One, two, three... One, two, three..."

She closed her eyes, feeling the room spin around her. Her body and mind were completely entrusted with Willem, and he held her with dignity and strength. Natalie had never felt so free.

"I promised you, Natalie," he whispered to her, and Natalie was pleased that she did not misstep as she listened. "You are as graceful and as beautiful as I knew you would be. All eyes are watching us. Everyone is envious. But I was wrong about one thing, Natalie."

"What is that?" she managed to ask.

"They are not envious just because you are dancing with me. They are also envious that I am privileged enough to dance with you."

There were no more words now – no more counting; no more flattering. There was only her hand on his shoulder and his on her back. There was only his hand holding hers and his breath on her neck. There was only contact – connection. Words were no longer needed.

As the music began its conclusion and Natalie opened her eyes, she stared into Willem's. When the music was no more, he bowed to her, releasing her hand for the first time since he took it.

That moment of broken connection made Natalie weak and hungry for more.

The many guests in the room began to applaud, but as Natalie's eyes darted across the faces, she could see many that were not smiling with their applause. There was a silent roar of jealousy that echoed throughout many of the more richly dressed young women in the audience, and that roar spoke volumes. For, as if it were the middle of the day at the marketplace and no masks were present, she could spot the vindictive stare of Sarah St. John.

The stare was ice cold, and Natalie wondered if Sarah recognized her as well. Whether she had or hadn't, Sarah's jealousy steamed through the room at her.

Natalie, turning away from Sarah's stare, bowed to Willem and nodded to the audience, all the while holding her smile steady. She would not allow Sarah to ruin this moment for her.

"I told you they would cheer," Willem said to her. His smile was larger than life. "They love us."

"Thank you for the dance," she responded in another half curtsy. "I truly had a wonderful time."

She did not wait for Willem to respond, and she moved through the crowd of people – away from the direction of Sarah St. John – and found another shadowed wall. This time, Willem followed.

"Did I saw something wrong?" he asked, touching her elbow from behind. Quickly, Natalie turned to face him. "Do you not wish for another dance right now? We do not have to dance – of course we don't. We can talk about whatever you would like."

"Would you not prefer a dance with one of the other girls here?" Natalie asked.

"I danced with many of those girls tonight, passing time until your arrival." He paused, but Natalie was silent in return. "Do you want me to dance with the other ladies?"

"It is your birthday celebration," she announced, forcing a new smile to appear. "I just fear that spending it with one girl will put a damper on it. I shall not be here late as it is. Tomorrow is my father's funeral, and there will be much to do come morning."

"Well, then," Willem said, catching Natalie's gaze with his piercing stare, "I imagine I had better enjoy what time I have left with you tonight. I may be privileged, but I do understand priorities."

"It will be a task learning how to function without my father," she replied, not having intended for the conversation to grow personal.

"I would be lost without my father," Willem admitted. "I have learned a lot from him, and I firmly believed that if he should pass and my family were to lose everything, I would be able to rise from those ashes. My father knows hard work, and I am not afraid to learn hard work."

These words were music to Natalie's ears. He had answered a question that she had earlier feared.

"Other people are dancing now," he added, and Natalie noticed that the music had begun again. "Perhaps this time, you and I can sneak into the crowd and join them. We would go unnoticed, I'm sure."

Although she was hesitant, Natalie grinned and nodded. Once more, Willem took her by the hand and led her, and as promised, they were able to slip in and disappear among the other couples.

She kept her eyes open this time. She was joyful and every move of her body felt as if it were guided by magic.

There was nothing about this moment that Natalie did not

love. She loved the feeling of having Willem embrace her body. She loved the way that he led her effortlessly from step to step, guiding her as one would the blind. She loved the way his breath on her neck gave her goose-bumps, and she loved the way he smelled of stallion and rose.

The only thing that Natalie did not care for was the one set of eyes that watched her. That set belonged to Sarah, who had locked onto her the moment Natalie and Willem had begun dancing again. This made Natalie shiver, as Sarah seemed more than simply jealous now. Sarah looked down right angry.

Natalie could only see her for a moment at a time, as her vision changed with every turn in the dance. Now, she saw Sarah whispering to a girl beside her – most likely her friend Victoria Luther. Victoria was also staring at Natalie now – and she was staring with eyes of scrutiny.

"Sir Willem," she asked, not breaking from the dance.

"Yes, m'lady?"

"Have you danced with Sarah St. John tonight?"

"With Sarah?" he asked, sounding almost appalled. "No, I must say I have not. She has cornered me with every opportunity tonight. She has been nearly impossible to escape. As a matter of fact, it was my father that insisted I invite her. He has dealings with her father from time to time."

"Why did you invite me?" Natalie asked.

"Because I wanted to get to know you better," he said, and her heart went all aflutter.

When the music ended and the partners had bowed, Willem took Natalie aside. Natalie noticed that Sarah's eyes still followed.

"I know that we have never spent much time together," Willem began, "but every candle in this manor was made by your father. He was a good man. He has supplied the Grilles Manor with candles for as long as I can remember."

"Yes," she said, "my father mentioned your father often."

"I remember seeing you," Willem continued. When I was a little chap, my father would take me with him to your local marketplace from time to time. I would see you at the counter, sitting atop it, greeting everyone who entered."

As he paused, Natalie did not know how to respond. She did, indeed, remember him, but she had seen much of the kingdom in that shop. She had not found the encounters substantial.

"You were marvelous. I remember your hair – red and curly. I remember how it was so wild and untamed. It was magical and it reminded me of fire. And your eyes – I remember the first time I ever saw them. I have never seen a pair of green eyes at all at that point, and never had I seen eyes that had sparkled with so much kindness and joy."

"I…" Natalie began, still unsure of what to say. "I am flattered by your words, Sir Willem. They do indeed honor me."

"You are worthy of honor," he replied. "Do you remember a few years ago, when your mother provided the cake for my aunt's wedding?

"Yes," Natalie laughed. "It caused uproar in the kingdom. Every village's bakers had sought that honor."

"My mother had to convince your mother to take the job," he added, "but I was thankful that she did. I intentionally rode with the servants to pick up the cake from your home."

"I remember that," Natalie said. "You did not speak a word the entire time."

"I went along only so I could gaze at you," he replied. "I had not counted on getting to speak to you."

This was too magical to be true, Natalie thought. For years now, Willem had been hiding a secret crush for her, and now he was letting her know. She felt weak at the knees, but she refused to let her body crash to the floor. She blushed, however, and turned her face to the side.

"Can I admit something else to you?" he asked her. His voice actually sounded nervous to her.

"You can admit anything to me."

"All of my life," he said, "I have dreamt of only one thing."

"And what is that, Sir Willem?"

"To know the feeling of your lips pressed against mine."

Natalie did not have an opportunity to respond, or even to consider what Willem was saying. She did, however, feel his hands as they wrapped around her waist, and she saw the tenderness in his eyes as he leaned into her. When his lips touched hers, she thought they felt soft and warm, like the silk that had been sewn into his costume. She closed her eyes, feeling her head spin and her world turn along with it, but she was not timid from it or threatened by it. In fact, it was the most wonderful thing that she had ever experienced, and as it was her first kiss, she was impressed with herself that it had been given by Willem Grilles.

She opened her eyes before the kiss was over, and she could see Sarah, still staring at her with the most terrifying eyes. Sarah's jaw was slack, giving her a disgusted look – even with her beautiful black and purple mask.

When the kiss broke, Willem took a small step back, giving some space between them.

"Was that alright?" he asked in a bashful voice.

"That was – wonderful," she answered with giddiness.

"Not even the fabled falls of Rah'moura Island could be as enchanting as you." His words were like the most luxurious velvet to her ears.

"Willem!" a voice called from somewhere near. Natalie looked to see Willem's father, Lord Charles Grilles, approach. "I have some very important friends here that I would like for you to meet."

Willem looked at Natalie and asked, "Do you mind?"

"Not at all," she said. "I will be right here waiting."

"I dare not keep you waiting long."

Natalie watched Willem walk off with her father, and glancing around, she noticed that Sarah was no longer watching her.

This gave her some relief. Natalie knew that Sarah had recognized her – she was certain of it. She wondered when – and if – she would confront her. There was also the possibility that Sarah had been upset by the kiss to such a degree that she had left the ball and was on her way home for the night.

That, Natalie knew, was just wishful thinking.

Waiting on Willem's return, she began to grow impatient. The music ended, and more music began. She could see him, but he was always surrounded by his father and his father's friends. It was good for him, she knew – meeting the right people. Yet, she felt alone again, and it was an uncomfortable feeling.

A dark shadow crossed over her and she looked up from the floor. A tall man of around six feet stood before her. He was wearing a dark red suit with a cream color, and his mask covered his entire face in crimson. His blond hair tied back behind his head.

"May I have this dance?" he asked her, extending a hand.

There was something familiar about him – something that she could not place. Regardless, Natalie seemed entranced by him and as she placed her hand in his, she let him lead her out to dance.

As he held her, their gazes locked and she could see his were as emerald green as her own. There was no timid nervousness with him. There was only an unusual familiarity – like she was in the arms of an old friend.

"You are ravishing," he told her. His voice seemed choked – nervous.

"And you, kind sir, look very entrancing as well."

Her words made him smile – finally forcing him to show her his impeccable grin.

"Do we know each other?" she asked him, curious as to who was behind the mask.

"Perhaps," he said, breaking eye contact, "but this is a masquerade ball. You and I – we could be anyone that we wanted."

"Who are you choosing to be tonight?" she questioned.

"I am choosing to be free," he answered, offering no further explanation.

Natalie smiled, wondering what he meant. Surely, a servant

would not have been so beautifully dressed. She could not fathom what kind of freedom this elitist was referring to.

Perhaps he had referred to the freedom from home or from his business, she imagined. It did not matter to her, really. This man – strong and tall – made her curious. She wished to see what was underneath his mask, but she knew she couldn't know – she mustn't know – as all identities deserved to remain a secret... hers included.

Their eyes connected again, and everything felt peaceful. She was not as wooed by this man as she had been with Willem. He did not tell her fantastic words that would send her into a tizzy. He did not point out that others would be envious of them dancing together. No, this was not dancing with someone new and exciting and eager to impress. This was dancing with someone so familiar that she did not care if people watched, and that made Natalie happy. Whoever guided her through this waltz was certainly a man that could see and feel her soul – not simply search for her heart. When the music ended, she was saddened, as she could have continued dancing with this familiar stranger throughout the rest of the night.

"Is this man bothering you?" Willem asked, stepping up beside her.

"What?" she questioned, startled. "No, of course not. We

were simply sharing a dance."

"I see," Willem continued, stepping in front of Natalie and facing the man. Willem stood a good four inches shorter, but he lean and strong – fearless. "What are your intentions with Miss Wills?"

"I only wished to dance with the lady," the man answered. His tone was low but held the presence of honesty.

"Well, the lady does not wish anymore of your company," Willem answered with a rough, cocky voice.

"Excuse me?" Natalie questioned. She was taken aback by the way Willem had spoken for her.

Willem held an arm out beside him, blocking Natalie from coming forward. "You come into my home, to my celebration ball, and you dance with my lady?"

Natalie could not believe her ears. They had spent a special moment together, but she had never told Willem that she was his.

"She was standing alone," the masked man replied. "I assumed that she was here without an escort, just as everyone here assumed that you were alone also. Many of these women around you danced with you earlier. I am sure this young lady does not mind even one of those dances."

"What business of yours is it how many maidens I've danced with tonight?" Willem was growing heated, and although still smiling, it was a gritty smile.

"Do not grow hostile," the stranger warned. "Hostility fuels fire."

"Gentlemen," Natalie pleaded, noticing that everyone around her was quiet. Looking at the crowd, Willem and the stranger had drawn their full attention.

Natalie felt a tap on her back. When she turned, she was faced with Sarah St. John. Without a word of warning, Sarah grabbed Natalie's mask and pulled it from her face, throwing it to the ground.

"I knew it," Sarah said bitterly. "You probably used witchcraft on Willem, just like you probably did on your hair."

"Witchcraft?" Natalie responded. She was growing tired of being called a witch. "My mother did my hair, repairing it from the travesty that Pierre had created."

Sarah lost her cool, drawing back one of her gloved hands and striking Natalie with a hard slap against the cheek. Natalie hit the ground, sore and stunned.

"You wretched creature!" the strange man growled, lurching forward. This seemed to entice Willem, who punched the man with as much force as he could.

"Natalie!" Willem shouted, after turning to see her lying on the ground. He looked at Sarah first, and then his eyes shot back to the man on the floor. "This is your fault! You did this!"

Willem was quick to his knees, straddling the man. He then punched him again – and two more times – across his masked chin. Natalie had no idea that Willem had such a violent streak – such a short fuse. She watched in horror as he fought the man who had only wanted a dance.

"See what you've caused?" Sarah said to her. You should have just stayed home, but this – look at what you have done. You've ruined everything!"

"I bet whoever you are, you're not so dashing now," Willem said to the man, taking hold of his mask and pulling it off. He pulled back and leapt off of him with terror.

"Devil!" Sarah shouted, seeing the face of the stranger.

"It's the beast!" announced Willem, climbing to his feet. "It is the monster of the castle on the mountain!"

Willem was smiling again, which terrified Natalie. She looked to the man on the floor below Willem – the man she had found familiar. Now, she understood why. Willem was exactly right – it was the *monster* of the castle, but he did not seem very monstrous to her in comparison to Willem's sudden rage.

She could see the hurt in the man's eyes – the pain and the embarrassment. As he began to stand, so did she, as if they were connected somehow by unseen mystical threads. The man, once on his feet, shielded his scarred face from the crowd as best he could, covering it with one arm while backing away.

"That's right," Willem said with a laugh. "Leave! Leave here, you monster!"

Natalie could not listen to this any further, and so she moved forward toward the man's defense. Sarah, however, grabbed her by the puffy sleeve of her dress, ripping it down her arm.

"Protecting a monster, are you?" Sarah chided in a threatening tone. "Only a witch would do such a thing."

"I told you she was a witch!" Sarah's brother Luke shouted from somewhere in the room. Then, he began chanting it. "Witch! Witch! Witch!"

Soon, others joined in. "Witch! Witch! Witch!"

Natalie grew even more frightened by this. The crowd was starting to close in on her with Sarah pushing on her and yanking more on the homemade dress.

"Enough!" the man they called *beast* shouted – high and mighty, his voice echoing throughout the room.

In a rush, he moved to Natalie and took her in his arms, pushing Sarah St. John off of her and onto the floor.

"Did you see that?" someone shouted.

"The monster – he just attacked Miss St. John!" added

another voice.

"Someone should stop that man!" cried another.

Natalie felt herself being lifted from the ground, secure in the man's arms. He carried her through the crowd toward the formal entrance. Several guests were already there however, blocking it from use.

"This will not be enjoyable," he whispered to Natalie – his voice calm and tender. "I will not hurt you."

"I know," she replied, although she didn't know she was speaking the words.

A testament to Willem Grilles' family wealth, a large stained glass window glistened from across the room. Natalie's eyes grew as she realized that was where this man was carrying her to. She closed her eyes tight and took a deep breath as he took a hard leap forward and plunged them through the window.

"They will follow us," the man told her, and Natalie knew that he was right. She could hear them at the window, and she knew it was only a matter of time before someone would catch up with them.

"My carriage," he added, setting her inside the passenger seat of a black carriage. He, himself, climbed on the front and grabbed the horse's reigns.

As he instructed the horse to go, it traveled with great

intensity, speeding down the hill. At the gate, Wilma was standing under the tree, but as the carriage sped by her, she followed right behind it – as if she had known Natalie was inside.

"Where should I take you," the man shouted into the air.

"Please do not leave me alone," Natalie pleaded. "They think I'm a witch. They will come for me."

She could hear them now in the distance behind them – men and women on their horses and carriages, shouting "Monster!" and yelling "Witch!"

Perhaps it was the darkness of the night, but Natalie could not tell which road they were traveling on. There were a few different routes into Foliage, and this one was more narrow and rockier than the rest.

"We will be safe in my castle," the man shouted, steering his horse up a hill and into a thicket of trees. The branches scraped against the sides of the carriage, terrifying Natalie further. She looked out the back, watching as Wilma kept up just a few paces away.

"They will come there!" Natalie cried, feeling doomed – dread swept undesirably across her flesh.

"They will not get in," he answered, but his words did little to calm Natalie's nerves. She knew that – if they did get inside – both she and the castle's lord were dead. Sarah St. John and

Willem Grilles would see to that.

14

They took a back entrance into the castle that Natalie had not known existed. She could barely walk as her legs were so unsteady when they arrived that she felt she would collapse. Her rescuer had taken note of her distress and had carried her inside, securing the stone door behind them.

"Can they break through that?" she asked, looking at the door.

"This castle has been through both war and fire. Nothing has brought it down yet," he answered.

He led her through what she had come to realize was the servants' entrance. They were in a hallway that had one doorway at the end. Once inside this door, the lord lit a lantern and shined light into the room. Natalie saw that they were in the scullery, and it looked to be the place the fire had started. Every bit of wood had been badly burned throughout most of the room.

"Wait here," he said, setting the lantern on the table and lighting a second one. He carried this one with him and disappeared from the room.

Natalie looked around her. She could feel the tragedy that had begun in this room. She could almost smell it – the burnt scent that followed a blaze of tragedy.

She wondered how the fire had started. Usually, there was no actual cooking done in the scullery. Had it been winter and a fire been going to keep the maids warm? She could imagine the sheer terror that the servants – and the family of the castle – had felt. She imagined it was similar to the fear her father had felt.

Perhaps, she thought, that this castle was a lot like her father's shop. Both had been greatly destroyed by the same element, so maybe a little love and care was all it would take to bring new life into them.

She imagined new tables and furnishings, new pots and pans along the wall... she thought of how grand it would be to see the scullery in action, the see the maids prepare courses that she had never even heard of.

Suddenly, she realized that she was imagining herself here – in the castle – living. Not visiting. Not helping around it. Living in it. Amazingly enough, the thought did not disturb her. It made her smile.

Natalie thought of the untold wonders of the castle – of all of the rooms and hallways that she had not yet seen and explored. She thought of the possibility of secret passageways, and she thought of a library – how grand a library a castle of this size must contain.

Her thoughts were interrupted as the lord returned.

"Come with me," he said, turning from the room again and leading the way.

Natalie followed, carrying along the lantern he'd provided her with.

He led her through the kitchen and into another hallway. From here, Natalie followed him to a large door. Opening the door, he let her step inside first.

Through the glow of the lantern, she could see it plainly. It was just what she had been thinking of – a grand library. Only it was dusty, ashy. It had also suffered from the fire, and most of the books and furnishings had been reduced to char.

She was devastated at the sight. Thousands of books, numerous pieces of art – all turned to rubbish.

"My father died in this room," he said, closing the door behind them. "This was his favorite room in the castle – it was his study. He had fallen asleep at his desk, reading one of his favorite books. I don't know if he felt anything. I was too young."

"How old were you?" Natalie asked, looking at the burned remains of the desk.

"I was three," he said softly. "I was asleep upstairs in my room. The servants said my mother left my side to rush down and help my father. She was crushed underneath a bookshelf when she came to his aid."

Natalie saw the fallen shelf. It was pushed onto its side. She wondered how many people it had taken to lift it, and if she had already been dead when they tried to save her.

"The servants fought the fire as much as they could. Several people from the village eventually came up to help, but they would arrive too late to save my parents. One of the servants knew that the smoke would eventually reach me in my room, so she took me in her arms and attempted to get me out of the castle. Near the bottom step, she fell and I went flying forward."

Natalie could picture the scene as he described it to her. It caused her great pain to imagine.

"I landed on the cold stone floor. I would have been okay, but another servant picked me up and ran. He was also trying to rescue me, but this is the one part of the story that I remember vividly. Someone – a man – held a large stone and struck the servant with it. As the servant fell to the floor, the man took me and brought me into this library, sitting me on the floor and leaving me to die."

Natalie watched as he wiped a tear from his eye. She could feel tears welling in her eyes as well.

"When the people from town arrived, the fire was at its worst. While they worked on putting out the first fires they came to, I was here, feeling the flames on my skin no matter where I turned or where I hid. I finally found solace in the far corner, where I laid down and went to sleep, prepared to die."

"What happened when you woke?"

"The fire was out," he whispered. "I remember everything being dark and hazy. My parents' bodies had already been removed from the room. If anyone had looked for me, they hadn't found me. If not for Madame Howell, I would have been as good as dead."

"Madame Howell?" Natalie asked, perking at the name. "What does she have to do with any of this?"

"She was the one who finally found me. She had come to the castle to bless it so that my parents' spirits could rest. She moved in after she found me, and she raised me as her own. She tended my wounds; she fed me and cleaned me. She clothed me and cared for me. She was as good of a mother to me as I could have asked for."

The lord continued to tell his story to Natalie, explaining that Madame Howell had kept his existence as much of a secret from the rest of the kingdom as she could. Everyone knew that his body had not been recovered from the fire, but no one knew that he still lived and breathed, growing older with each passing year – just as those below the mountain did.

"People began to suspect something from Madame Howell," he added. "She had tried to only go to and from the castle at dark, either early in the morning or late in the evening. Yet, as she began to age, this grew hard for her. Suspicions began to arise, and the townsfolk had begun to think that she was using the castle for some evil witch stuff – nonsense made up in their own wild imaginations."

He was quiet for a moment. Natalie tried to read the expression on his face. He was no longer hiding it from her, and she could see every scar left by the miserable fire. Beyond that, she could see the pain that still remained in his eyes. She could feel his hurt. Gently, she reached to him and placed her hand on his.

This startled him and he stood, nearly falling back.

"I'm sorry," she said. "I did not mean to frighten you."

The lord huffed, looking at the floor. "I imagine I'm more than a bit jumpy right now. Waiting is painful to me. Waiting on the crowd that followed us feels like it did when I watched the village leaders approach the castle, cornering Madame Howell out front of it. They had shouted at her – screamed at her. They had accused her of everything and anything they could, and they had made her fall to her knees in tearful fear. I watched from my upstairs window for as long as I could, but rage had filled me and once I was outside, I was on them like a wild animal in the jungle.

I cut them and scratched them, bit them and punched them – I was beyond angry. I'd had enough of the cruelties of the world. It took everything I had in me, but I managed to scare the crowd away from the castle. I was then known as the Beast of the Castle, but I preferred to consider myself Madame Howell's protector, as I've been watching over her ever since."

The lord was quiet again, but only for a moment. Softly, he added, "That night, she promised me everything would be okay again – that I would be okay again. She promised that one day my scars would heal – both inside and out. I did not believe her then, and I am not sure that I believe her now. Still, it is a fascinating thought."

"I am terribly sorry," Natalie said, as she found it hard to digest all of what she had just heard. "What you have gone through – it is horrendous. How, I wonder, did such a fire spread through this castle so quickly?"

"I've never understood it," he said in a deep whisper. "The layout of the castle… it was almost as if each room had been lit individually. I was too small to remember, but so many different scenarios have filled my mind over the years. All I know is that it was intentional. I can feel it in my gut."

"Who could have done such a horrible thing?"

"Somebody who held a grudge against my father, I'm

assuming. My father was a great businessman, and he had made many enemies along with his acquaintances. My father was very prominent in the kingdom. The only family crest that rivaled his in financial success was the Grilles'."

Natalie was silent as she thought of Willem's reaction when he saw who was under the lord's mask. He had acted out of spite and anger – fire sparked by a long family feud.

"When did people come to realize you were still alive?" she asked him. "Why have you remained here, locked away?"

"I am not locked away," he began. "I choose to be here. And they have known about me ever since that day I protected Madame Howell. I protect her, and she protects me. They stay away and afraid. They whisper terrible stories about us, but they leave us alone otherwise."

"Until I came into the picture," Natalie whispered. "I have caused you so much trouble tonight."

"Miss, the trouble is just beginning."

"Natalie Wills," she said with a strong but smooth voice. "My name is Natalie Willis. I do not have a title. My father was a candle maker and my mother takes odd jobs cleaning, sewing and baking. We have always struggled to make ends meet, but we have always managed. My father died in a tragic fire just a few days ago. His shop burned, and he was trapped inside. His service is tomorrow."

She said it all so fast that it came out on one long breath. She wondered why she had said so much. All she had intended on telling him was her name.

The lord looked at her, as if judging her character by her outburst. Then, he bowed before her. Rising, he said, "It is a pleasure to make your acquaintance, Miss Wills. I am Lord Roger Holloway, III, sole heir to the Holloway estate." Looking around, he held his hands up. "It may not look like it, but I come from a rather privileged lineage."

As he smiled, Natalie could see the humor behind his introduction. His smile, she thought, was beautiful. It was somewhat animalistic – clean and full but with the presence of small fangs that glistened from the light of the lantern. She smiled in return and looked away toward what remained of the books on the shelves. For a moment, she wondered if there was anything worth salvaging. Then, as the sound of her name being screamed from outside the castle walls distracted her, she decided reading would be better suited for another day.

"Natalie!" the voice screamed again. Although it was faint from where she and Lord Robert were, she could still make it out – it was Willem Grilles. "I've come to rescue you from the beast, Natalie!"

"What is wrong with that man?" Lord Robert asked, irritated.

"We're going to burn you, Natalie!" she heard another voice shout. This one was distinctively that of Sarah St. John. "We're going to burn the witch!"

"I don't feel safe here," Natalie said, looking at Lord Robert. Lord Robert took his lantern and beckoned her to follow him.

"I know where we can go," he said, "but we will have to do it fast."

He led her from the library to the front foyer of the castle. There, Natalie could see blurry images of people through the narrow windows. Several of them held torches, and although the light helped to illuminate them, she could not make out any of their faces. They all seemed to still be wearing their masks.

A start jumped through her as they began knocking and banging against the door. A large wooden slate secured it, but Natalie wondered how much pressure it could take before they broke through it.

"Come out, Natalie!" Willem shouted from the crowd. "Or let me in! I can save you from that disgusting beast!"

"Come on," Lord Robert ordered, taking her hand and leading her away from the entrance. He took her down another hallway and, midway through, he stopped. She watched as he opened a door and she followed him inside. There, Lord Robert moved to a candelabrum on a far wall and twisted it. Natalie's eyes grew large as she watched a bookcase slide to the side, opening a secret passageway.

While still afraid, she was also excited.

The secret passageway opened up to a tunnel that led them between the walls of the downstairs rooms.

"I have not been in this passageway since I was a child," Lord Robert confessed, moving slowly. "This should lead us back to the kitchen."

"We're going back to where we began?" Natalie asked. The fear overshadowed the excitement completely now.

"They are all at the front entrance. They will not look for us out back."

A sudden crashing sound could be heard in the distance. Natalie knew what it signaled – the mob had broken through the front entrance.

"We must hurry," Lord Robert directed.

"I thought you said that door had withstood war and fire," she noted. "How did they break through?"

"I said the castle survived those things," he remarked. "I never said anything about the door."

Natalie rolled her eyes at this, but there was no time for debate. They were running through the walls while an unknown amount of people searched the castle rooms for them. She was terrified and felt like a mouse being sought by a cat.

"Maybe we can talk to them," she said. "Maybe they will listen."

"Quiet!" he ordered. "They could hear us."

"Natalie!" she heard Willem Grilles shout from a room nearby. "I know you're in here, Natalie. There is nowhere to go. Please, come out."

"Witch!" she heard people shouting, and it chilled her to the bone.

Once again, Natalie had managed to place herself in an impossible situation. The only person she could trust in the entire castle was right here with her, and it was the man that most of the village feared the most.

They travelled quietly. Lord Robert led her on some unsuspected turns through the passageway and when they reached an end to it, they stood before an old stone wall. Natalie looked around, holding her lantern in every direction she could, but she saw no door – no exit to salvation.

"This is a dead end," she noted, feeling any shred of hope that had clung to her fade away into the shadows. "We're trapped."

"Ye of little faith," Lord Robert said. He then knocked on the stone wall three times, in three different places. It began to separate in the center, sliding to the sides. It was yet another secret door, and Natalie was astonished.

This door opened up to a dark set of stairs. Cobwebs shielded the entrance.

"Hurry!" Lord Robert said, pushing through the cobwebs and leading the way. "The door shuts after thirty seconds."

Natalie heard the door start to rumble, and quite slowly, it began to close. With a leap, she moved through it and onto the first step. The door shut tightly behind her.

"When your entire life has been spent inside of one building," Lord Robert acknowledged, "you learn its secrets and its mysteries."

"Where will this lead us?" she asked him.

"To the roof," he said. "It's the only safe place I can think of right now."

The stairs wound up and around in a tight, claustrophobic space. Natalie ran a finger along one of the stone walls, feeling a trail of dust collect. She took her finger away – not that it mattered. Every step she took, another cobweb clung to her hair and dress.

"Once we're out of the bastion," Lord Robert added, "it is important that you mustn't speak. We mustn't let them know where we are."

Natalie did not respond, but she understood. From the roof, there had to be another area to escape to – otherwise Lord Robert would not have been leading her there.

At the top of the bastion, Lord Robert unlatched and pushed open a heavy door that led onto the rooftop. He took Natalie by her hand and led her out onto it.

Willem Grilles, Sarah St. John, and around a dozen other masked people awaited them.

"Do you honestly think you are the only one that knows the secret passages of this castle, beast?" Willem asked Lord Robert. "My father knows the insides and outs of this castle like the back of his hands."

"What are you talking about?" Lord Robert asked.

"Surround the beast!" Willem ordered with the grimmest of smiles.

Lord Robert watched as several of the people – many with torches – approached him and backed him against the rounded wall of the bastion. Natalie hurried off to the side, where she was faced with Sarah St. John. Sarah moved closer toward her, and Natalie backed away.

"My brother says he tried to get you to fly, witch," Sarah said, and she stopped moving once Natalie was at the edge of the roof. "You would not do it for him, but I imagine I can persuade you."

Sarah lunged forward, placing her hands on Natalie's shoulders. Natalie screamed out, fighting the girl but unable to push her away.

"Sarah, I have grown tired of your childish games!" Willem shouted, marching up beside the girls. He took Sarah by the waist and – without hesitation – flung her over the edge of the roof. Her scream was brief, cutting to dead silence as she hit the ground.

Everyone present became hushed. Natalie's eyes darted to Lord Robert. Although he was still kept at bay, Willem's entourage stared at him. Natalie was certain they were as shocked as she was.

"Sarah has been a thorn in my side for many a year, Natalie," Willem told her, touching a finger to her trembling cheek. "Perhaps this time, she took the hint."

"Why are you doing this?" Natalie asked him. She felt too close to the edge and was afraid that she would be next thrown over.

"Don't you see, Natalie?" Willem continued. "You and I were meant to be together. I've been watching you since we were children, waiting for the day when we could be joined. But, your father needed you, and you and your mother needed him, so I helped us out and did to your father what my father did to the beast's years ago. Father told me just how to do it – how to make you mine."

"What are you talking about?" she demanded, growing more angry than afraid.

"My father removed his nemesis through fire," Willem said. "I found his method to work very well."

"You killed my father?" she asked him, feeling the rage as it boiled beneath her skin.

"What can I say?" Willem asked with a laugh. "It runs in the family."

From behind Willem, near the bastion, she could hear Lord Robert roar out in a sound that could have only been made of both pain and uncontrollable anger. She watched him as he tore through the crowd of people that held him at bay, throwing some to the side as if they were made of paper, and punching others so hard that they fell to the ground unconscious. Two tried to climb onto his back, but Lord Robert threw them from him as if they were weightless paper dolls. He was clearing a path and making his way to Willem. His eyes were animalistic. Smoke rose around him from the fallen torches. Natalie was certain that vengeance would finally be his.

Willem turned in enough time to see Lord Robert approach him and grab him by the collar of his suit.

"I should throw you off of this roof right now!" Lord Robert told him, spitting in his face. "I should end you the same way you ended that girl."

"Sarah?" Willem laughed. He still appeared fearless. "She was nothing but a waste of breath. The vultures will enjoy her more than you or I would."

Natalie took a step back as Lord Robert raised Willem off the ground, dangling his feel over the ledge.

"You won't do it," Willem said, shaking his head and smiling. "You don't have a deadly bone in your body. The rest of the kingdom may fear the great beast, but I know the beast is nothing but a mere pussycat."

Natalie wondered how true this was. Would Lord Robert prove the kingdom to be correct about him – would he prove that he was a beast? Or, would he show himself to be the man that she knew him to be and turn him into the Royal Guards for a just punishment?

Honestly, Natalie did not know what decision she would make if placed in the situation. She could actually imagine herself striking revenge for her father, and she hoped that Lord Robert would not be the same.

There had simply been enough death.

A moment passed, and as Lord Robert began to lower

Willem, he threw him off to the side, down to the cold ground of the castle roof. Natalie felt relief as she watched him. He hung his head low and looked over the roof's edge.

"I am not you," Lord Robert said to his enemy. "I am not a beast."

"No," said Willem, standing on his feet once more. "You do not have the strength to be a beast. You, dear lord, are a coward."

Natalie gasped as Willem plunged toward Lord Robert, pushing him over the ledge of the roof. Lord Robert managed to grab hold of part of Willem's jacket, bringing him over with him. With one hand, Lord Robert clung to a stone – the only thing separating him and Willem from their deaths.

"Don't let go!" Willem shouted, showing fear for the first time.

"I cannot hold on," Lord Robert whispered, looking only at Natalie as she stared down at him. Natalie watched as his fingers began to slip from the stone, and with every ounce of strength and might that she had, she grabbed hold of his wrist. However, the weight of both Lord Robert and Willem Grilles was too much for her. She began to lose her grip, just as Willem's jacket began to rip.

"No!" Willem pleaded at the sound coming from his

clothing. "No, please! You mustn't let me fall!"

Neither Natalie nor Lord Robert had a choice in the situation. Willem's jacket tore, and as it did, he fell with a piercing scream and plunged to his death.

Natalie cringed as she heard Sit Willem's bones shatter on the rocky mountainside, but she could not tear herself away from her current task – the task of helping Lord Robert back onto the rooftop. She felt relief as she saw the hand he'd held Willem with grab hold of the stone wall. As he pulled himself up, she pulled also, and he was quickly saved. It was then that she saw he still held part of Willem's jacket. Once Lord Robert was on his feet, he dropped the fabric beside him and looked breathlessly to Natalie. Natalie rushed into his arms, holding him tight.

"The beast," one of Willem's entourage said as they started climbing back to their feet. "He killed Willem!"

"The bugger deserved it!" replied another one. "Did you see how he threw Miss Sarah off the roof?"

"But the witch," said another. "She must have made Sir Willem behave in such a way."

Natalie and Lord Robert broke their embrace, and once more, she felt nervous. They watched as the group of people gathered together into an angry mob. Yet, before they could take a step toward the couple, a sight Natalie could have never imagined appeared.

Slowly descending from the sky, Madame Howell – dressed all in black – landed on her feet and stood between the group and the couple.

"Yes," the old woman said with a nod. "Witches can fly, and we can do a lot worse than that."

With her back to Natalie and Lord Robert, she took slow steps toward the suddenly frightened group of torch-bearing thugs.

When Madame Howell was just a few paces away from the group, she threw her hands into the air. Glittery, sparkling dust swirled through the air, all around and over the group. Their torches fell to their sides.

"You will remember from this night only the facts," the old woman whispered to them – her voice like the hissing of a snake. "You will remember how Willem Grilles sent Sarah St. John to her death. You will remember how Willem confessed the murder of Hiram Wills and of his own father's murder of Lord Roger Holloway, II. You will remember how Willem trapped and attacked Miss Natalie Wills and Lord Roger Holloway, III, and you will remember how Willem had, in the end, been responsible for his own death. All else that you have seen here tonight – including myself – you will forget."

As she lowered her hands, Madame Howell turned toward

Natalie and Lord Robert. She smiled at the one she had secretly considered her own child, and then she nodded a head to Natalie.

"You had better be on your way home, young lady," she told Natalie in a pleasant but firm tone. "Tomorrow will not be an easy day, and your mother will need you fresh and at her side."

"Father's funeral," Natalie whispered. It had all but slipped her mind.

"I shall take you home," Lord Robert told her, but she shook her head in decline.

"I have Wilma with me," she answered, looking at him. "She and I will be fine." When she looked back to Madame Howell, the old woman was gone. "Where did she go?"

"She has a tendency to pop in and out as she pleases," Lord Robert laughed. "But she is a kindly old witch, and I love her."

The crowd of Willem's flunkies stared around at each other in confusion. They all admitted to knowing what had happened with Willem and Sarah, but none of them could recall much else of their visit to Holloway Castle.

Natalie felt no fear from the crowd now, and she left with them, through another doorway several feet away from the bastion. This doorway had been how Willem had led them to the roof. Now, it would be the way they would depart it without him.

Outside, Lord Robert helped Natalie atop Wilma. He stared

into her eyes, smiling a look of thanks.

"I am indebted to you," he told her, taking her hand. "You have helped me solve a family tragedy that has plagued me for most of my life."

Natalie understood his sentiments. She now knew that her father's death had not been an accident. He, like Lord Robert's father, had been murdered at the hands of a Grilles family member. The thought sickened her, but for her father's death, justice had come.

"I am equally as indebted, Lord Robert," she confided, "in ways that you may not imagine."

And this was true, for if it had not been for Willem's brutal attack on Lord Robert at the ball, she would not have seen the grim, dark side of a young man whose obsession with her had begun with stalking her since they were children. She also would not have known the truth about what had happened to her father.

She smiled at Lord Robert and nodded her head. Then, with a command and her heel pressed into the Dales Pony's side, she and Wilma rode off into the dark of the night, leaving the myths of the castle beast in their trail, knowing that the beast was already dead.

"Long live Lord Robert Holloway, III!" she shouted into the night, loud enough for Lord Robert to hear. "Long live the

Lord of Holloway Castle!"

* * * *

Once home, it was nearing sunrise. Roselyn sat in her chair by the fireplace. A look of impatience was plastered across her face. As Natalie entered, Roselyn did not move. Natalie could barely tell if she was breathing or not.

"Wilma did not buck me off one time," she told her mother. "She was wonderful tonight."

"You are home mighty late," Roselyn told her. The voice was flat but held concern.

Natalie could see no point in putting this conversation off, so she sat at her mother's feet and told her the story of the ball, and the brilliant dances that she had shared with both Willem and a masked stranger. But then she had to tell her mother the hard part and the truth behind who the beast of the castle really was and of how her father had not simply died, but he had been murdered.

The tale was lengthy, and the sun had fully risen when Natalie had concluded. Her mother had traveled through a series of emotions, from sadness and tears to anger and disbelief. She had shown fright, and she had shown thanks. Natalie could read all of this on her mother's face, as her mother did not speak a word during Natalie's entire story.

When all that was to tell had been told, Roselyn finally spoke again. "So," she began, running a hand over her daughter's head, "witches really can fly, huh?"

They both laughed at this, and Natalie was thankful that her mother had not lost her sense of humor throughout all of the tragedy of late.

"I understand now what you meant, Mother," Natalie told her. "Willem was the most beautiful man, but inside, he was the greatest monster that there was."

"He was the spawn of his father," Roselyn noted. "I am certain that everything he learned, he took from him."

Natalie could see a bit of anger sweep over her mother's face, but she knew that her mother had earned that anger. Whereas Natalie had lost a father, Roselyn had lost her husband – the love of her life – all because of a psychotic, spoiled boy.

Resting her head in her mother's lap, Natalie closed her eyes and drifted to sleep. She remained this way until Roselyn finally woke her to prepare for Hiram's funeral service.

15

Lord Charles Grilles had not yet received word of his son's demise at the time of Hiram Wills' funeral. He had, however, displayed the audacity to attend the funeral – perhaps if only to see if Natalie had survived to attend. Roselyn had earlier told Lord Jensen of Lord Grilles' and his son's terrible deeds, and as Father Harris said a prayer for Hiram, the Royal Guards of the King arrived, leaving with Lord Grilles in shackles.

Although it had caused a scene at the funeral, Natalie had found it appropriate – as it had given her father a sort of redemption and public justice before his peers and his family.

Lord Jensen had kept his word to Natalie, and in the weeks that followed her father's service, a team of skilled carpenters worked to repair and rebuild the Wax Shoppe. Soon, the building was ready for use again, and Natalie had decided that she was ready to work.

News of the Grilles family scandal had spread like wildfire, and the Wills name had gotten a much needed boost. On opening day of the new Wax Shoppe, it seemed like half of the kingdom had shown for the event. Natalie felt herself overwhelmed with business, even though she had made a huge stock of various candles to provide to her customers.

As the day grew long, she and her mother tidied up the mess from the foot traffic, took note of the remaining inventory and prepared to close up shop.

The bell above the door jingled as it opened. Natalie looked up from the counter to see Lord Robert enter the shop.

"Well, hello," Natalie said, smiling at him and offering a half-curtsy.

"Miss Natalie," he said, nodding his head. Looking to her mother, he added, "It is a pleasure to see you, Madame Wills."

"The pleasure is all mine," Roselyn said, taking her broom and moving to the back of the shop. Looking to her daughter, she added, "I'll finish closing up."

As Roselyn disappeared to the broom closet, Lord Robert approached the counter. He picked up a lavender candle and looked at it.

"Smell it," Natalie said. She waited with baited breath for his reaction.

"It smells wonderful," he replied, exhaling as he set the candle down.

"The smell is lavender," she told him. "The same as its coloring."

"Madame Howell is preparing our supper right now," he

said, "but she promises to disappear whenever we arrive."

"I do hate to rush the poor dear out," she said, stepping from behind the counter and taking Lord Robert's hand. "Let us give her some extra time."

"What do you have in mind?"

She led him from the shop and through the marketplace. There were few people out now – mostly merchants closing up their shops. Natalie continued to lead him beyond the marketplace and to the fountain that offered the most brilliant view of his castle.

"This is one of my favorite places in the entire world," she told him, running a hand through the fountain's water.

"Why is that?"

"Because," she said, looking up to the castle, "I know you're always right there, and if you are there, I know I'm always safe."

She turned to him and brushed his long blond hair away from his scarred face. Then, pulling him to her, she gathered all of the bravery she could muster, closed her eyes and kissed him. It was their first kiss, and it was sensational. Never had she felt such warmth and tenderness – such kindness. She felt a sort of electricity surge throughout her body, and she curled her toes. Once their lips parted, she took a step back and looked into his emerald eyes.

Then, her eyes grew wide with surprise and she took yet another step back. Natalie raised a hand to cover her mouth – as if she was about to scream.

"What is it?" Lord Robert asked her. There was a tinge of panic in his voice.

"Your face," she whispered, pointing at him as she lowered her hand. "Your face."

Touching his hands upon his cheeks, his expression also turned to awe and surprise. His face was pure again – flawless and beautiful. There was not a single scar there – not one sign of the fire that had burned him so badly many years ago.

"Could it be?" he asked with great emotion. "Could you have fulfilled Madame Howell's prophecy?"

"Your scars – you're healed," Natalie whispered, and her expression turned to one of happiness.

"Because of you," he told her, stepping closer to her and taking her hand. "Only someone who loved me for who I am inside could have fulfilled Madame Howell's promise to me. I am no longer a beast!"

"You never were," Natalie told him, and once again, she kissed him – tenderly, with deeper passion than before.

Once the kiss broke, they walked hand in hand up the mountainside and to the castle, where Madame Howell had prepared their supper.

16

Lord Robert looked to Natalie, who was sound asleep on the chaise lounge across the room from him. He sighed, half pleasantly and half through sadness.

He had learned to accept that she loved him, and he felt the same for her – with all of his heart. Yet, there was something that disturbed him. Something deep within that he could not pinpoint – could not quite put his finger on. He watched her eyes move beneath their lids. She was dreaming, and he wondered if it was a dream about him – about them and their new life together.

Three months had passed since the unraveling of the treachery surrounding his parents' deaths. Robert had come to terms with it now, and he had been able to finally put their spirits to rest, but it had all seemed so easy – so theatrical in a way – that he had a trying time comprehending it. The thought that a family could have destroyed by such cruelty was beyond him.

But this uncertainty – this lack of stillness within him – had little to do with his parents. Instead, it was brought forth by and focused upon that young lady sleeping before him, resting peacefully without a care in the world.

Natalie had been true blue to him. She had been fearful at

first, but she had learned to see beyond the scars that had riddled Robert and had looked into his soul, finding the real him – the one that had been lost all those years ago.

So, why was it that, after all was said and done and they were soon to be wed, he still could not fully trust her?

She was an innocent young woman. She'd lived a modest life with a humble family, and as far as he knew, Natalie had never done a thing to intentionally harm another. And, despite his flaws and grimaces, she seemed to love him.

He stood from his chair and crossed to the window, turning his back to sleeping Natalie. Staring out into the crisp fall scenery, he considered Madame Howell. Madame Howell more than approved of Natalie; she had served as an instigator in their relationship. Madame Howell had cared for Lord Robert over the years as if he had been her own, so he had no reason to doubt her loyalty toward him or to question her approval of Natalie.

Perhaps, he thought as he turned from the window and looked at the sleeping beauty on the chaise, the problem lay within him and not with her.

It was not that he didn't love her. He *did* love her. He owed her so much, for without her, he never would have learned the truth behind his parents' deaths, and he would have still been a scarred outcast hiding within the chambers of this castle. Yes, he loved her with all of his might, but did he love her like she deserved to be loved? Like she *needed* to be loved?

Her eyes opened and she stretched. When she saw him looking at her, she smiled.

"I must have fallen asleep," she said in a tired tone of voice.

"This castle is wonderful for one thing only – sleeping. I did nothing but sleep here for years." He smiled in return, showing that his words were made more of humor than anything else. "You slept through lunch. Would you like for me to prepare you something? I got a fresh side of ham from the village market just this morning."

"I must have dozed while you were gone. Did you stop by the Wax Shoppe? It is Esmeralda's first weekend alone."

"Esmeralda is fine," He told her, sitting beside her as she lowered her legs from the chaise. "She's been apprenticing under you for several weeks now. It is time to let her work a day or two by herself and allow you to get some much deserved rest."

"I had a dream," she said, stiffening as she looked down to her knees.

"Congratulations," he said and grinned at her. His smile fell away when he saw she wasn't wearing one. "I'm sorry. That was inconsiderate of me. What was your dream about, my love?"

"I dreamed that you were gone," she told him, raising her eyes to meet with his. "I dreamed that you had left me."

Taking his hand and placing it upon hers, he felt a cold tremor down his spine as she slid her hand away. "We are to be wed in just a few days. Where would I go?"

"That's just it. In my dream, you left me alone at the wedding." Her voice was flat and her emerald eyes pierced him to his core. He looked away, down to the floor, and then off to the window.

"It was a dream," he said, finding his voice through the thick knot that had suddenly grown in his throat. "Cold feet, perhaps. Nothing more. I would never do that to you – embarrass you in such a way. No gentleman would."

"And you are a gentleman," she acknowledged. A slight smile grew upon her lips. "You have welcomed me into your home. You've cared for me, helped me with my family's business... We have shared secrets and stories – the most intimate details of our lives. You are the best friend that I have always wanted."

"But?"

"But I worry that perhaps, just perhaps, we should *stay* best friends?"

He heard it in her tone, that her statement was more than a

statement; it was a question. She had doubts, and it seemed likely that she was picking up on his doubts also.

"I have just come of age," Natalie said, standing and crossing the room. "And you. You have been sheltered here your whole life, shunned for your appearance and more or less banished from society. Now, you are free to roam and celebrate across the lands, and not a single soul will judge you. You have a brand new life that could lead to doors you've never known."

"And what of you?" he asked her, standing from his spot at the foot of the chaise and moving to her. "Have you not a new life also? A new journey into business, a freedom from your enemies, and a castle that is as much yours as it is mine?"

"It just all seems so sudden… so coincidental."

Lord Robert opened his mouth to speak, but he found that he was unable to counter her. What Natalie said spoke to the heart of what he had been feeling. Every single bit of it had felt to him like it had been pre-destined… pre-determined.

"It feels like…" he began.

"A fairy tale," she concluded.

There was a moment of silence – so thick that it made the air hard to breathe. Just as they were looking at one another, albeit in a daze of confusion, they turned from one another. Something was amiss; something was just not right.

"Why would Madame Howell not have simply fixed your burns when they occurred? Why make you wait to find true love?" Natalie's words beat into his brain so hard that it made him wonder if his ears would begin to bleed. "Why would she have made you suffer for all these years?"

"Why did she choose you to give that mask to?" he said after a pause of hesitation. "None of this feels right."

"It doesn't feel real."

Normally, Robert knew, that when couples said things like 'this just doesn't seem real,' that meant they were happy in their bliss. He and Natalie, albeit suddenly, were not happy. They had been mindlessly playing *couple* since the night of the masquerade ball. There had been no troubles, no drama, no bickering, and no consequence for anything in their prior lives before that night. It was too perfect. Too much like a *happily ever after*.

They turned toward each other again, stared into one another's eyes, and almost simultaneously, they said, "I can't do this anymore."

17

On horseback, Lord Robert rode Natalie to the foot of her mother's property. There, he took her two satchels and set them upon the dusty ground; it was as far as she wanted him to go.

"I do love you," she told him, touching his face and kissing his cheek. "And you are the greatest friend I have ever known."

"I love you," he whispered back, looking from her stare to the ground, the horse, the sky – anywhere. Without another word, Lord Robert climbed atop his handsome horse and trotted away. He did not look back to Natalie, and he knew that she would not look back at him. Their time together had come to an end.

When Natalie and her home were far behind him and the village was in sight, he tied his horse to a hitching post and took the cobblestone walk by foot. He intended to pay a visit to the woman who had been no less than a mother to him – Madame Howell.

It was Saturday and the village marketplace was bustling. He'd ventured here only hours before, to gather the fresh ham and some other goods for he and Natalie to enjoy over the weekend. Now, that idea was far away; the food would be indulged in solitarily… eventually… maybe.

He strolled through the crowd of people with his chin up and his shoulders strong. He was on a mission, and as the occasional villager greeted him, he offered none of them no more than a nod of the head. He was not arrogant; he was not unkind or unfriendly. He was simply in a hurry.

He could see the wooden sign for Madame Howell's Shoppe of Wonders hanging from its hinges on the post outside the shop. He felt his pace quicken. The closer he drew to it, the faster his heart seemed to beat, his head to spin, and his stomach to churn. When he reached the shop and turned toward the door, he reached out with a hand that quivered and trembled as it had never done before. Looking at his hand, he could see former scars from a fire long ago begin to show again, blurring in and out repeatedly.

He opened the door and stepped inside, but the place was dark and smelled like musk. There were cobwebs hanging all around, and as he stepped through, he walked through those cobwebs no matter which way he turned. He had been in this shop only two days ago, and it had not been anything like this. It felt as if it had been long abandoned.

"Madame Howell?" he asked in a voice that felt dry and childlike. The words barely came – almost a whisper – but they arrived nonetheless. "Madame Howell, are you here?"

There was no answer. Only the echoing of stillness could

be heard once his voice faded. Despite the fact that there were dozens of people outside at the market, he could not hear a sound from them inside this building.

"Madame Howell!" he yelled, finally finding strength in his voice. "It's me, Madame Howell. It's Robert."

Still, there was no response to his call and he found himself walking toward the backroom where she was known to be when there were no customers in her store.

"Madame Howell, I have some questions that I need to ask you. Please. It's important to me."

He opened the curtain separating the shop from the backroom and stepped through. Letting the curtain drop behind him, he sealed himself off in a new darkness. He seemed to be in a hallway – narrow walls stood on either side of him. He walked with slow, cautious steps, feeling for a door but finding none. The hall seemed to continue on several feet, and he knew for a fact that Madame Howell's building was not much deeper than the shop inside. In fact, it was the smaller of the buildings on this side of the village square.

Yet, this hallway of closed-in blackness seemed to carry on until finally his hands pressed onto a wall in front of him.

There were no rooms in this black hall – no room for potion making, or crafts, or even storage. Yet, he knew this was her backroom – where she went when there were no customers in the shop, but it made no sense. Where was she? Where was anything?

When Lord Robert turned back, all he could see there too was blackness. He knew that the curtain had to be somewhere; he simply couldn't see it. Yet, he walked steadily, continuously – feeling ahead of him for the curtain, traveling several more steps than he had when first entering this hall of blackness. No matter how far he walked, he could find no curtain, just a continuance of the hall until, at last, he touched upon something – another wall ending the hall. The curtain was gone.

"Madame Howell!" he shouted, beating upon the wall with fists of fury, hearing his own voice echo throughout the darkness around him. "Madame Howell! Let me out of here!"

18

Roselyn let go of her daughter after a hug that seemed to have lasted forever. Natalie was in absolute tears – distraught, emotional, and vocal about her choices.

"No," she said, correcting herself, "it wasn't a choice, Mother. It was a set-up, by that wicked gypsy witch."

"Madame Howell?" Roselyn asked. Her voice was nurturing but it did not sound convinced. "How did that old lady ruin your relationship?"

"She didn't ruin it. She created it!" Natalie's words come out as more of a shout now, although that was not her intention. "She could have healed Lord Robert from the beginning. She always had the power to do so."

"Maybe he had to learn something important?" Roselyn questioned. "Perhaps he had to first find someone who loved him for who he was?"

"Yes! That was the witch's game from the get-go!"

"Game?"

"Oh, Mother, you just do not understand. Madame Howell gave me an enchanted mask, knowing very well that it would lead me to Lord Robert. But there was no true love, Mother. There was love, yes, but it was a friendship love. Anything that we felt was because of a series of events, all set off by Madame Howell."

"I think you are putting too much into this, lass."

"You've seen her power. You and Father – you drank the wine she sent you."

"Oh, but before we ended up in that tree, your father an' I had the best night of our lives." She smiled fondly and grew quiet. Natalie could see that her mother was reminiscing over her own true love.

"Do you not understand that nothing Lord Robert or I did was of our own free will? We were led to each stage of this – each predicament. Why? Why would Madame Howell play us like puppets?"

"So the old woman played matchmaker. I think it's sweet, personally. And the two of you did seem pretty happy together. I think Madame Howell did a fine job."

Natalie noticed her mother's smile, the tone of her words… everything was blank – but flowery.

"I still say you are overreacting, Natalie." Roselyn took her hand and led her into the kitchen, to the table. When they sat, she continued. "You found true love! How splendid is that! And it seems that, aside from your own suspicions, everything was working out happily ever after."

Natalie stared at her mother in disbelief. She stiffened in her chair and looked Roselyn in the eye. "What did you say?"

"Oh, everyone deserves a happily ever after! Even you!"

"Do you believe in fairy tales, Mother?" Natalie stood from the strong oak chair and backed away toward the cutting table. "Do you believe in *happily ever after*?"

"I believe in you," Roselyn said, walking toward her with a steady grin plastered upon her full, nurturing face. "And if Madame Howell had a hand in making my baby girl happy, then I believe in her too."

Searching for an escape from this moment – from her mother and from this house – Natalie walked toward the door and into the sitting room. In a moment, she was at the front door.

"I have to go," she said, not looking back to see if Roselyn was still in the kitchen. "I just remembered, there is something I have to do."

"Return to your Lord!" Roselyn called to her as she stepped outside. Her voice seemed different to Natalie now – aged far beyond her years.

She shut the door between them.

She moved with a hurried stride. Yet, it seemed the further she got from the house, she could hear her mother's voice louder with each step.

"Return to Lord Robert!" and "Return to your Lord!" were repeated over and over, and even as her swift walking turned into a run, she could not shake the words.

Eventually, she came to a dead stop and dropped to the ground, having to cover her ears and close her eyes in an attempt to block out the roar of her mother's voice, flooding her mind with a great deafening echo.

"Stop!" Natalie shrieked.

And then there was a silence, but it was a deathly silence and once that frightened her. With the calming of her mother's words, other things dissipated all at once. There were no more birds singing their melodious songs. There was no breeze to blow through her hair or the leaves of the trees. There were no signs of insects, cattle or horses. The air was thicker; it felt as dirty to her as it smelled. Something was wrong in the world, and it extended far beyond the threat of a forced happily ever after.

Frightened and pushed to a new limit she had not before experienced, Natalie was back to her feet and running with all her might. She ran until she reached the foot of the village, and she relaxed when she saw people again.

Just up ahead of her was Mrs. Hillbrooke and her daughter Gwendolyn chatting on the side of the road by their home.

"Mrs. Hillbrooke!" Natalie called, finding new strength and

running up toward them. "Gwendolyn! Mrs. Hillbrooke!"

Neither of the two ladies responded to her, but as Natalie drew closer, she wondered if they would respond to anything. They were statuesque – immobile and breathless. Frozen in a moment in time with Mrs. Hillbrooke in mid-laughter and Gwendolyn with her lips parted – perhaps in the middle of a sentence. It was uncanny, and it frightened Natalie more than the earlier echoing of her mother's aged voice.

She continued on, noticing the same statuesque theme with each person she came across on her way. No one spoke; no one moved. No one breathed.

"This cannot be real," she whispered, turning in a circle as she came to the market and finding dozens of villagers frozen in their moment in time. Some appeared to have been talking amongst themselves – some yelling. Children were in mid-play near the courtyard, and one man was in mid-fall from a punch, thrown by another man; he, too, seemed to be frozen in a fall caused by the strength of his swing.

Had everyone been moving and speaking and breathing, it would have seemed like just another day in Foliage.

As she walked through the stationary villagers, she felt as if she was the only person in the world. It was the eeriest, most cryptic feeling Natalie had ever experienced, and it made her ache inside. When she reached the Wax Shoppe, she stepped inside and looked for Esmeralda.

The shop was a mess. Esmeralda had, with obvious clumsiness, spilled several batches of wax on the counter and the floor, and had left it to dry. She, herself, was nowhere to be seen. Perhaps she had taken leave after her mess-ups, embarrassed to tell Natalie what had happened.

Natalie would have understood, she thought as she stepped through to the small office and supply room where her father used to keep books.

Something went wrong with her eyes for a moment... her ears. A flicker of light – different colors scrambling and clearing. Blink in; blink out. A buzzing in her ears, brief but prominent, and then all was clear again. The shortest moment, the shortest flicker, but its impact was great, for when Natalie entered the room, she found her father sitting at his desk, counting out his day's earnings.

"Father!" Natalie cried, rushing up to him and pulling him into her arms. Yet, as she hugged him close, she realized that her beloved father was no different than any of the people she'd seen outside as he too was motionless, wordless, and breathless.

She released him and stood upright, taking soft steps back.

Tears began to well in her eyes again, but she fought them back with as much strength as she could muster. She was trembling, but she was determined to be bold.

There it was again, just as her boldness struck – the flicker, the buzzing, only this time it was more intense and the buzzing rang so loudly that it sent her to her knees in pain. She covered her ears and pressed hard, and in a moment, the buzzing stopped and only remained as a reverberant, painful echo in her head that finally sank away.

When she opened her eyes again, her father was gone and Esmeralda was in his chair, sleeping with her head on the desk.

Natalie stood and dusted herself off. She tried hard to stop the trembling that cruised throughout her body, but her skin crawled and her teeth rattled against each other.

She did not bother to try and wake Esmeralda. She had a feeling it would do no good. She also decided then and there that Esmeralda would no longer be working at the Wax Shoppe once everything was back to normal… if everything ever got back to normal again.

She left the office, stepped through the shop, and ventured outside, where everyone was still just as she had left them.

Her next stop was to pay a visit to Madame Howell.

19

Lord Robert's knuckles were bruised and bloody from pounding on the walls in hope of breaking through them. He had given up for the moment and was slumped against one of the black walls catching his breath and gathering his thoughts.

His breath came to him in time, but his thoughts were something else completely. He remembered many distinct things – he remembered the fire, and how things were grand and glamorous before. He remembered what his parents looked like, and he remembered time going by as slow as snail and as quick as a flash of lightning. He remembered having birthdays, but he did not actually remember the events themselves. He remembered Madame Howell caring for him, but he remembered no specifics.

He distinctly remembered Natalie visiting his castle, and his fondest memory was returning her mask to her in the middle of the night. He remembered the ball, and he remembered the devastation that followed.

He remembered that he and Natalie had been together for three months, but he remembered little of the events of those three months. This morning, he had ventured to town for a ham and other goods, but what about yesterday? Had there been a yesterday? Yes… he knew it had to be so. But what had happened yesterday? Specifically, what had he done?

In short, Lord Robert felt as if he was losing his mind. He had to be. There were no other explanations; none that he could conceive. He was going mad, and the longer he remained in this long black hallway, the madder he would become.

Perhaps, he thought, he'd already gone mad, and that this really was Madame Howell's backroom, only he *thought* it was a black hallway with no doors that had trapped him within it.

If that was the case, then this wall that he was leaning on wasn't really a wall. It must have been the curtain that he had entered through, so in theory, all he had to do was acknowledge that the wall as a curtain and he would be able to exit through it.

Lord Robert stood from his slumped position on the floor, propped up by the wall, and he turned to the wall and stared it right in its blackness.

"You," he began, talking directly to it, "are not a wall. No. You, my friend, are a curtain!" He said the last part with great emphasis and flicked his fingers at it, as if performing wizardry. Then, holding his head high and smiling wide, he walked right into the wall.

Robert stumbled backward. He had hit the wall hard, and it dazed him.

"No," he whispered, bowing. "You, my friend, *are* a wall."

He gathered himself and decided that his earlier assumption was wrong. The wall was not really a curtain, and he was still trapped in this forsaken hallway.

He felt like a prisoner and it was a feeling he had once been accustomed too, when he had felt trapped in his own home – a shunned, scarred reminder of a horrific, tragic event. He had not felt like a prisoner since Natalie, though, and the thought of her made his heart warm.

Suddenly, the warmth that came with the thought of her turned cold as fear sashayed in. If he was being held prisoner here in this hallway of darkness, what horrors must Madame Howell have been putting Natalie through in the meantime? Was Madame Howell putting him out of the way while she dealt with Natalie? And if she was... why?

"Madame Howell," Lord Robert announced, keeping his voice as calm as possible, "you must free me from this prison. I have done nothing to harm you, and neither has dear Natalie."

He waited for a response – *hoped* for a response – but when one did not come, he paced the floor in consternation.

There had to be a way out. That was the logical part of him talking. It seemed to be the most trustworthy voice that he could listen to right now, and so he focused. Only magic could have trapped him in a hall like this one, and magic was nothing more than an illusion. That right there, he thought – that was logic.

All of this meant that the hallways itself was, indeed, an illusion, and all he had to do was break through the illusion. This, he decided, would be a lot less painful than breaking through the wall that he'd tried to make a curtain.

He tried to focus on the hallway and to imagine it transforming into Madame Howell's backroom, where he would be able to exit through the curtain. He focused... focused... focused... nothing.

In a bout of frustration, he prepared himself to shout words into the emptiness that would have made even the most experienced woman blush. Yet, before he could release this storm of obscenities, his vision faltered. There was a flash – quick as light, but built of multiple lights, colors, static. There was a buzzing – a sound that accompanied it. From the flicker, Lord Robert became temporarily incoherent and disoriented, but once the buzzing died away, he found his senses returning to him.

Looking around, he watched the flicker, which seemed shift from hallway to shop repeatedly – sporadically. He was still there – in the shop; he could see it now. He could see through this illusion that had been built around him, and he yearned to escape it. Perhaps, he thought, if he stepped through the wall during the flicker, he would return to inside the shop.

Deciding one more hard impact with the wall would not do him too much more harm, he went for it – timing his walk as best he could with the sporadic flickering – and once the flicker revealed the shop interior, he stepped ahead.

This time, and much to his delight, he did not nearly knock himself out. This time, he was in the shop and out of the horrid hallway.

All around him, his world continued to flicker. Things around him shuffled and changed, as if searching for their own identities, attempting to remember what they were supposed to be.

The sight of it all was dizzying, nauseating, and it made Lord Robert wobbly on his legs. It was as if the world was going out around him. With the flicker now came flashes of white and black, causing everything else to vanish for instances.

He looked to the exit – watched as it flickered – and he charged for it. When he reached the wooden doorframe, he felt as if he had to brace himself with it and pull himself through, as the shop seemed to not want to let him leave. However, as he stepped outside, he saw that it was not just the shop; it was everything. Everything flickered – the people, the buildings, the wares and produce. Only one thing did not flicker and that being was approaching him with swiftness. Through the erratic nature of the world as he knew it blinking in and out, he barely recognized his own Natalie.

20

When she saw him, she knew there was hope. She watched him move, even though his movements seemed forced and almost helpless. He was struggling just as she, fighting against this ferocious change in their worlds. She went to him, held him in her arms, and led him away from Madame Howell's Shoppe of Wonders. The place, she decided, was wicked – although she knew nothing yet of Lord Robert's experience within it.

"There is nowhere safe!" she shouted, as she felt she had to. The buzzing from the flickers and shifts was near deafening.

"The castle!" he told her, pointing up to their castle on the mountain. Madame Howell had repaired the castle from its damage after Natalie and Robert had their *happy ending*. Now, however, it looked worse than it had when Natalie first ventured up to it. It was shaking – rattling – and chunks of it were falling off, far down to the ground below.

"It's too dangerous," she responded, shaking her head.

"It's where we first met," he told her in a voice that was loud and firm, but also somehow romantic to her. "It's the only safe place!"

She felt his words to be true. She held his hand and

together they walked against the shifting plane of reality, onward and upward toward the castle. Beneath their feet, the mountain seemed to crumble, making their climb more treacherous and frightening than ever before.

"Hold on to my hand!" Lord Robert yelled and she tightened her grip on him, feeling his warmth as he led her forward.

All around, a musky wind began to blow, ripping around them and flinging flickering stone, dirt and trees in all directions. But there it was – the impending entrance to the place where Lord Robert had spent the most secluded years of his life.

Until she appeared. Until Natalie stepped through his threshold and into his life.

Natalie mustered forward with all her might, knowing she had to. Not for herself, but for him, as he had risked all in protecting her at the ball, and she owed him the same. If she could not protect him, she could at least be with him.

Now, in this seemingly endless moment of rampage and terror, she remembered why she had given him her heart to begin with. He was a beautiful spirit that made her feel like the most important person in the world. To her, that made *him* the most important person in the world.

The door crumbled away before their eyes and they stepped

into the castle with quickness and care, dodging a mass of falling stone.

"Now what?" she asked him with pleading eyes, although she knew that this was all a mystery for him as well.

"We wait."

"For what?"

"For her."

The tone of his voice scared Natalie more than anything else. It was a tone she'd never heard him use before; it was the voice a child would use – a child who was afraid but was trying oh so very hard to be brave.

"Look at all that I have built for you," a voice echoed amongst the howling wind and buzzing flickers. It was a distinct voice – kindly, aged. It belonged to Madame Howell, although Natalie did not see her anywhere. "Look at how you are so carelessly tearing it all apart."

"How are we doing this?" Lord Robert shouted, searching for her but finding nothing more than crumbling rubble.

"I gave you everything!" the voice continued, although this time the tone was more harsh than kindly. "I created this whole world for the two of you, so that you could have a happily ever after! Oh, it sounded so romantic! And then you two had to go and ruin it all."

Every word that Madame Howell spoke – whether she stood in front of them or not – infuriated Natalie more than it confused or intrigued her. She had so many questions, and the witch was dancing around her words.

"You owe us an explanation!" Natalie shouted, still searching the castle interior for a sign of Madame Howell's physical self.

"I owe you nothing!" arrived the response in a tone no less than demonic. "I am your God!"

Natalie could feel the power of the witch, and she knew to practice caution as she spoke, but she felt that she had to press into Madame Howell in order to make her show herself.

"What kind of God," she began in a voice as loud as she could carry, "is afraid to show itself? Have you only your magic powers when you're safe and hidden?"

"Natalie!" Lord Robert said, tugging her arm. "What are you doing?"

She looked at him and smiled. Her emerald eyes melted into him, and her touch to his hand was warm and caring. "We are ending this. Now," she told him, bravely.

"You deem me afraid?" Madame Howell asked in a thunderous voice that shook the castle more than the rippling flickers of reality or the onslaught of the ferocious winds. Then, a white cloud formed before Natalie and Lord Robert, and it slowly expanded, growing into the size of a shorter, plumper person. Before their eyes, Madame Howell materialized. "Is this better? Do you prefer this form, my dears? The kindly old lady approach? Does this appease you?"

At the sight of the old woman, both Natalie and Lord Robert were rendered speechless. Although Madame Howell looked quite like her usual self, she seemed to glow with a green aura that surrounded her and filled the air around her with the stench of decay.

Natalie could feel the trembles over her flesh blend with those covering Lord Robert, and yet she stood strong and looked at the woman with stone cold eyes.

"How dare you interfere with our fates," she began, intending to cut the woman down with her words, but her words were cut short instead.

"Your *fates*?" Madame Howell asked. A bellowing, harrowing laughter followed her words, sending a frost of terror straight to Natalie's soul. "You have no fate, my child. You have only my whim. I have told you; I am your God."

"You may have had a hand in bringing us together, but I assure you – you are no God."

"And I assure you," Madame Howell told them in a soft

tone, "I am your God."

When Natalie tried to speak again, Madame Howell threw up her withered hand, silencing the young girl. However, Natalie was not silenced by force of threat or by relinquishment. She had no choice but to remain silent, as if an invisible set of stitches ripped through her lips, sealing them tight from any movement.

Natalie felt panic ripple through her. Her stomach churned, her legs felt weak, and she was more nervous now than she'd ever been. She'd felt she had to stand up to Madame Howell – to get reasons, excuses, facts and responsibility – but now she wondered of Madame Howell's harmfulness and magical abilities far beyond the young girl's own understanding.

Lord Robert, in an attempt to verbally defend Natalie, found himself in a similar state but one a little more immobile – unable to talk, and suspended several feet in the air inside a bubble. Lord Robert's lips were not sealed, no words came out. He could neither cry for help nor demand the witch's surrender – either of which he knew he was unlikely to obtain.

Madame Howell circled around Natalie and stared up at Lord Robert. Natalie had her eyes clamped shut; Robert's were pleading.

"I had higher hopes for you than this," Madame Howell told Lord Robert. She smiled at him but her voice was sad. "I had higher hopes for both of you. You see, I always wanted a family. Demons cannot bear children, you know, and so I had to create my family. But I did not want just *any* family. I wanted a strong, nurturing family – one that had suffered plenty at the hands of others and had still managed to find it in their hearts to accept and love others. Isn't that a beautiful thought? A beautiful ideal? So, I created you – both of you – and everything and everyone you have ever known. Your parents, your friends, your enemies."

Crossing back to Natalie, Madame Howell flicked her hand upward, forcing Natalie to open her eyes.

"Yes, I created you – the unlikely farm girl who would rise above her mediocre place in the world and find her prince." Glancing to Lord Robert, she added, "And you. Somebody so broken by the hatred and cruelty of others that you were assured to fall in love with the first pretty, friendly face that you saw."

Even if Natalie could have spoken, she did not know what she would have said. None of what Madame Howell was telling them made sense, but as she tried to think back over her life, she found that there were many more gaps in her timeline than she had ever realized.

"All either of you had to do was enjoy your happily ever after. That's all I wanted. Oh, you cannot blame me for being a romantic at heart. I gave you everything, but it was not enough."

Madame Howell looked as if she was almost about to cry, but her crinkled face turned to a smile. She walked back to Lord Robert and looked at him with the kind eyes of a grandmother or a favorite aunt. She sighed and turned her back to him.

Natalie, through confusion, sadness and anger, considered her father and his merciless death at the hands of fire. She looked at Madame Howell, wondering how anyone could have put a kindly old man through that sort of torture.

She took her eyes off of Madame Howell and away from Lord Robert to focus again on their surroundings. The wind had grown even stronger as Madame Howell's disappointment and anger grew. The castle continued to crumble around them; there was nowhere to turn – nowhere else to go. It was an impossible situation, Natalie thought, but then again, nothing truly seemed impossible anymore.

"Now," Madame Howell continued, "we can forget all of this ugliness and return to how things have always been – you two madly in love in your castle and me just a kindly old shopkeeper – or I can start from scratch. I hate the idea of losing the two of you, but if I have to, I will gladly dissolve you and start with someone fresh."

Natalie's eyes grew wide at her words. What did that mean – "dissolve?" The thought made her blood run cold.

She caught Madame Howell's eye and the woman approached her and stroked her trembling cheek. Natalie stiffened, too terrified to move.

"You look like you have something to say, my dear," the old witch told her. Then, running a finger along Natalie's lips, Madame Howell allowed them to part.

Natalie swallowed hard. She had to find her voice. She had to speak but her mouth was dry and her tongue was thick and it felt like her throat was on fire from some internal flame that was trying to encompass her. She opened her mouth, but instead of words, she coughed, hard and harsh until she was brought to her knees from the painful misery of it. Madame Howell looked at her, smiling gleefully over her suffering, but this reminded Natalie of the newfound anger that she held inside for the old crone, and she brought herself back to her feet.

"What do you mean *dissolve*?" Natalie asked her, impressing herself by the sudden and appreciated arrival of her voice.

"My child, it does not matter what term you use to refer to me by. Some have called me a witch. Most have penned me a demon. Others have bowed to me as a God. It does not matter, as my power cannot be measured by title or greatness. You, Natalie, and you, Robert – and everything and everyone you have ever known – are nothing but a spell that I casted to entertain myself. You never existed before that spell, and you will cease to exist when I dissolve it. Every experience you have ever had is because I created it for you."

It could not be true. None of it could be true. Natalie was certain in her heart that the old witch was lying, attempting to further raise her upper hand in the situation. Still, Natalie knew the pain that she felt when her father died in that horrible fire. She knew the sadness and the embarrassment struck upon her by Sarah and the betrayal of Willem. Those were emotions that she herself had owned and held. Witch, demon, god – it did not matter. No one could control how she *felt*, no matter how much they had controlled the situations around her.

How she *felt*…

Her own words struck her like a bolt of lightning. She looked at Lord Robert, who remained helpless inside a bubble, and she remembered how she had *felt* around him. She had loved him, more than as a best friend. The problem had not been with him, or with her for that matter. The problem had been with their life – with the pre-determined existence that surrounded them. They had needed adventure; adventure was what had brought them together, and why they had fallen in love in the first place. And now, standing where she was, facing the ultimate fate of an impossible and seemingly irrepressible doom, Natalie gazed into Lord Robert's eyes and knew without a shadow of a doubt that she was still – very much indeed – in love with him.

"My Lord," she said, letting everything around her disappear in her mind and only him remain.

Lord Robert looked to her. His eyes met with hers and they grew calm from the chaos around him and the captivity that held him tight. His mouth fell slack and he no longer seemed to fight against the bubble.

"I love you, my Lord," Natalie told him, as loudly as she could, but her voice refused to be a shout. It was as serene and blissful as a sunrise over the meadow in the springtime. "I love you with all of my heart and all of my being!"

She watched as Lord Robert lifted a hand and touched his heart. Then, he brought the hand to his lips and kissed it. Slowly, his hand moved toward Natalie and pressed out to her as far as he could reach. She reached back desperately, knowing it was impossible to connect with him physically from where she was standing, but she tried nonetheless.

"Enough of this rubbish!" Madame Howell shouted, stomping her foot on the castle floor and bringing about an eruption of energy that caused the mountain itself to quake. Everything shook harder around them than before, and the exterior walls of the castle crumbled completely away. The mountain, itself, began to further dissolve outside. "You *had* your chance, and that chance is over! The time for *I love you* is over. It's time to say *goodbye* now."

Natalie backed away from Madame Howell as terror returned fully to her bones. She watched as the woman turned and faced Lord Robert and slowly began approaching him. Whereas the noise around them was shattering, she could distinctly hear every word the withered old woman spoke.

"You shall go first, young Robert," the witch told him as she lifted a hand and extended it toward him. "I had such great care for you. I built you a remarkable storyline, and I gave you such great wealth. You appreciated none of it – nothing I did for you. I brought you *true love*, and I even gave you a happily ever after. Did any of that please you? No. You are ungrateful and ignorant. Real, *true* mortals – they would have given anything to have what I've given you. You are selfish… a mistake in my spell, and I shall remedy that right now."

Natalie saw Madame Howell's hand begin to glow. The glow began white, but it quickly transformed to red. Her fingers flared out; nails as long as knives grew sharp as the blades they resembled. Natalie knew what would happen when Madame Howell brought her hand down. It would cut through the bubble that trapped Lord Robert, and it would likely slice through him as well.

Whereas, just hours ago, she was ready to walk away from Lord Robert, right now she felt that she would do anything to save him... anything to keep him near and safe. That, if nothing else, was the definition of *true love*.

Doing anything sometimes meant to sacrifice one's self, and Natalie was prepared to do just that as she charged Madame Howell from behind, tackling her away from Lord Robert and onto the crumbling floor. With Madame Howell's fall, the world around them shook with even greater force, and the ground around them crumbled into a black pit of nothingness, nearly claiming them with until it halted as Madame Howell caught her bearings.

"Foolish child!" the old woman shouted in the deepest, most demonic tone that Natalie could have ever imagined. With a swoop of the hand, she flung Natalie across the room to one of the few remaining walls. The wall crumbled from the girl's impact, disintegrating into nothing. Madame Howell turned to her and began to walk toward her. "You think you can stop *me*? I am older than time, girl. I am your *creator*!" Her voice echoed, hard and mighty, shaking what remained of the structure and the mountain around them. "I am eternal!"

Natalie looked behind Madame Howell to see that her fall

had broken the spell that had entrapped Lord Robert in the bubble. He was rising from his fall after regaining the freedom of his limbs. Just as Natalie had done, Robert charged at Madame Howell, knocking her from the path to Natalie. Once more, Madame Howell fell to the ground, and once more the ground around them fell into nothing.

This time, Madame Howell did not respond with an insult or a threat. She responded with a shriek as deafening as anything Natalie could imagine. The young girl held her hands to her ears to try and block out the sound, but she found the challenge an impossible one. Pulling her hands away, she noticed that they were covered with blood. Madame Howell's shriek was making her ears bleed.

As the shriek concluded, Madame Howell climbed to her feet once more, staggering over toward Lord Robert, who was still floored from his tackle. Natalie took this as a sign that it was her turn, and she again charged the demonic creature. This time, however, when she contacted with Madame Howell, they began to roll. They rolled over the few meters of floor that remained, and as Madame Howell toppled down onto nothingness, Natalie groped desperately to cling to a bit of floor and keep from falling to her doom.

She could barely hear the screaming of *no* as Madame

Howell failed to secure herself on anything and tumbled far into the blackness that she had created.

Natalie struggled to hold on to the one castle brick that she could cling to. All around her, bits of the castle continued to fall away, and she knew that it was just a matter of time before she would be taken too.

Then, out of the darkness that filled her eyes, she saw her Lord Robert as he reached down for her, taking her by the wrists and pulling her up to him.

"Quick," he told her, leading her from the edge. "To the center."

"My Lord, even with Madame Howell gone, everything is still crumbling away. What is happening?" Natalie was frightened, and she held on to Lord Robert as if he was a part of her own being.

"Everything she told us must have been true," he said, holding her tight as they stood in the center of the room and watched everything spin, crumble and disappear around them. "And if that is fact, then we have broken her spell."

Natalie looked at him; her green eyes were filled with fear of the unknown. He pressed a hand to her cheek and stroked it.

"Then… then that means…" she began, but he placed a soft finger over her lips to silence her.

"Do not say it," he replied, putting on a strong face and a tender smile. "All that matters is us – you and I – right here, right now."

"I love you, my Lord," she told him, fighting back tears.

"I love you, Lady Natalie, for now and forever."

Leaning into her, Lord Robert kissed her with such tenderness melded with such a passion that Natalie felt her fears melt away. They held this kiss – their final kiss – until the floor that crumbled became no more, until the mountain ceased to exist, and until they – themselves – began to flicker and fade away. And even then, their kiss did not break. For them, their final kiss would be a kiss that lasted into all eternity, frozen in time, unknown to all but the two that mattered… the two that had shared it. And aside from that unbeknownst memory, as Lady Natalie and Lord Robert flickered one final time and disappeared into a blackness that they no longer feared, nothing else of their world remained.

Epilogue

The sun was shining. The sky was the softest blue, and birds were singing the most melodic songs that the ear could ever know. Spring was the favorite season of Julia's; she loved it with all of her might. Despite the fact that it meant a sometimes overwhelming amount of hard work on the farm, the beauty of spring far made up for it.

Today, she had it fairly easy. Her father was in a neighboring village with her brothers purchasing supplies for the farm, and her mother had been too caught up in baking to want to break away for the daily shopping, so Julia had been given the task. She did not consider it a chore, because she thoroughly enjoyed the village market. Although somewhat small as compared to some of the neighboring villages, Wenten was as charming as they came.

The marketplace, as she had expected, was booming with villagers – both selling their wares and purchasing. As she passed through crowds of people, she spun and smiled while she gazed upon them. The excitement of the bustle thrilled her to no end. Deep inside of her, there was a girl who yearned for adventure away from her family farm – that dreamed of excitement and exploration – but the girl in that fantasy seemed destined to find those thrills in the activities of others, which was why she was an avid reader.

Julia read anything and everything that came her way, soaking up knowledge, adventures, dangers, and stories of true love every opportunity that she could. Her father and mother had encouraged her yearning for literature, and she knew – without her father even telling her – that when he and her brothers returned home, her father would have a new book for her.

Wenten, however charming it might have been, was not a very literate community. There were few books to be found, aside from the *good book* at the small church at the foot of the village.

One by one, Julia gathered the small amount of items on her mother's list. A bundle of white yarn from Mrs. Whipple's sewing supply stand and a small basket of sunflowers and a mixed bouquet of fresh flowers from Mr. Jameson's market stall.

As she sniffed the fresh flowers, letting their sweet aroma envelop her, she looked ahead to the corner of the marketplace. There sat a small shop that she had never dared to venture into before. It was quaint and charming, but there was something about it that had always made Julia feel nervous and uneasy. It was a curiosities shop that had stood there for as long as she could remember, yet for the life of her, she could never remember seeing anyone enter or leave the shop at any time.

Julia stiffened and grinned from ear to ear. She held her shoulders back and slowly began to stroll toward the shop of curiosities.

"Today's the day," she whispered as she walked. "Today is the day that I have an adventure."

When she approached she shop, she stopped and took a deep breath. Then, on the exhale, she pushed the door open and stepped inside. A bell rang upon her entry.

On first glance, she saw no one – neither customer nor clerk. The store, however, was filled with so many wondrous oddities that it swept her away. There were things so foreign to her that she wondered where they could have come from, as she couldn't imagine anywhere on Earth creating such things. There were terrifying wooden masks, dolls made of cloth and hair, jars, bottles and vials that contained goopy, leafy or powdery substances that made her cringe, and there were things that had to have been pulled straight from nightmares.

Then, there was the other side of the merchandise: beautiful fabrics of silks, satins and velvets, gorgeous jewelry displaying the finest of a variety of stones, candles that were scented with the most relaxing of aromas, and so much more that it was both overwhelming and intriguing.

"Can I help you?" a voice called from somewhere toward the back of the shop.

Julia felt her heart jump at the shock of the sound. She gathered herself and cleared her voice to speak. "I – I am wondering if you might have any books?"

"Books?" the woman asked as she appeared through a door from the backroom. The attendant was old and withered, but very grandmotherly – a nurturing sort. "Ah, you are the literary type, I see. Well, come here, my dear, and let me see what I can find for you. As you can tell, I have so much merchandise that my old mind has trouble remembering what I actually have amongst it all." The old lady laughed, and Julia laughed along with her.

"You do have a lot of *unusual* things here."

"This shop is a trove of treasure, I tell you." Turning down an aisle, the woman stopped and pointed to the furthest shelf. "There. That's where the books are kept. You may browse them as you like."

"Thank you," Julia replied enthusiastically. With obvious eagerness, she hurried over to the books and browsed. There were four rows of books and they were all titles by authors she had never read before. She could not remember the last time she felt so excited.

"You may have any book you choose," the old woman

stated from the end of the aisle.

"Oh, I couldn't ask you to part with your merchandise without compensation," Julia said, although the offer had been generous. "It would not be fair."

"Then you will return each book when you finish it, and take another in its place." The woman paused to take a breath. "I have not sold a single book in this village. I might as well keep up that tradition."

Although Julia still found the offer overly generous, she accepted and chose her first book to borrow. She brought it to the clerk and showed her, happy to see the clerk smile at her choice.

"An adventure book," the old woman said. "You do seem like a lass that enjoys a good adventure."

"Adventure, romance, suspense – I love it all," Julia told her in a giddy tone. "Between you and me, I sometimes fantasize that I am a character in one book or another, getting to live their adventures and excitements. Can you imagine what a life it would be, to be a character in a book?"

"Oh, my dear, you have no idea the adventures that await you." The old woman's smile grew larger. Her eyes were bright behind their spectacles. "I am pleased that you came into my humble shop today. Please, in honor of our new acquaintanceship, let me give you a token of my appreciation."

"I couldn't possible accept anything more than what you have already given me," Natalie said, holding the book close in her arm with the flowers. "You've been awfully generous to me."

"Please, my child. I was beginning to feel like a neglected old woman. Let me have the opportunity to feel like a loving grandmother."

How could she argue with that? Julie suddenly found herself unable to resist the woman's offer, and her eyes grew wide with awe and surprise as a necklace was presented to her. The necklace itself glistened like authentic gold, and the stone in the center was the largest, most flawless ruby she had ever seen. Six diamonds outlined it for effect.

"Oh, no," Julia said, shaking her head. "That – that is much too extravagant. I just couldn't."

"What am I supposed to do?" the old woman asked her. "Take it with me when I die? I have no one to leave it to, so I would like for you to have it. Please, grant an old woman's wish. Take the necklace. For good luck."

"For good luck?" Julia repeated as she allowed the woman to place it around her neck.

"For good luck," the woman repeated. "When you wear it, you will open yourself up to the most exciting, wonderful adventures."

Julia wanted to laugh, but she dared not insult the woman. Instead, she thanked her bashfully and accepted the gift. As she began to leave, she turned to the old woman and asked her, "What is your name? I am sorry. I forgot to ask before."

"My dear child," the old woman said, approaching her, "you may call me Madame Howell. Remember that name because I feel that you and I will be seeing a lot more of each other in the future."

"Well," Julia said, stepping outside, "thank you again, and I promise that I will visit you again soon – and exchange this book for another."

"Goodbye, my dear."

As Julia turned away, holding her new book, wearing her new charm, and carrying her mother's goods, she thought of how peculiar the old woman had seemed – and this thought would have been increased had she turned around. Then, she would have seen Madame Howell watching her as she departed, smiling wide and eagerly, with her eyes glowing with the redness of Hell. Julia would not have known exactly what was happening, but she would have at least had a clue – a tip – that Madame Howell was anything *but* a kindly old woman. Madame Howell was eternal, and with that fire of immortality, she was the greatest evil that Julia could have ever encountered, far surpassing any antagonist from any book that she could have read. She would have had the gut feeling – the undeniable instinct – that Madame Howell was a puppeteer, tugging at the strings of a village full of hapless marionettes. However, had Julia known that Madame Howell was both her creator and her enemy, she would have never had the chance of the newfound adventure that awaited her around the very next corner that she would turn down. She would never have the chance to meet the handsome Lord that was meant to be her one true love, and she would never seize the opportunity – the destiny – to experience her very own happily ever after.

The End

Additional Releases from Jae El Foster

Restless

Where the Demon Is

Shaded Whisperings: Forever

Shaded Whisperings: Playing St. Nick

Kings & Queens (DCL Anthology)

Enchanted Fairy Tales (DCL Anthology)

Visit Jae El Foster online at

www.jaeelbooks.com

www.ingramcontent.com/pod-product-compliance
Lightning Source LLC
Chambersburg PA
CBHW031609240626
47153CB00002B/683